THE
RED PETTICOAT
Joan E. Palmer

ILLUSTRATED BY W. T. Mars

Lothrop, Lee & Shepard Co.

NEW YORK

Copyright © 1969 by Joan E. Palmer
Library of Congress Catalog Card Number: 71-81928
Printed in the United States of America
1 2 3 4 5 73 72 71 70 69

To my mother and father,
and to my husband,
who helped and encouraged me
to write this book

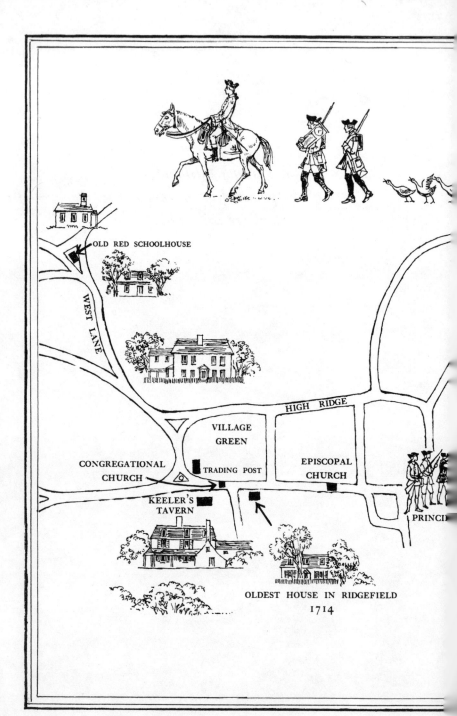

OLD RED SCHOOLHOUSE

WEST LANE

HIGH RIDGE

VILLAGE
GREEN

CONGREGATIONAL
CHURCH

TRADING POST

EPISCOPAL
CHURCH

KEELER'S
TAVERN

PRINCI

OLDEST HOUSE IN RIDGEFIELD
1714

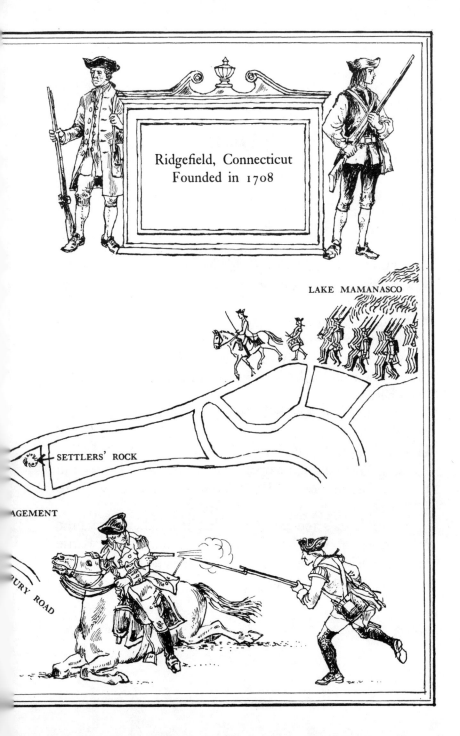

Ridgefield, Connecticut
Founded in 1708

LAKE MAMANASCO

SETTLERS' ROCK

AGEMENT

BURY ROAD

Introduction

The historical detail in this story is true. As students of the American Revolution know, the Battle of Ridgefield took place on what still is the main street of this charming New England town, and a number of rebel homes were burned on that tragic day in April 1777.

And if you should visit Ridgefield today, you would see, still standing, many of the landmarks that were a part of the town when the heroine of our story, Eliza Bouton, lived here.

You could see Keeler's Tavern, much as it was almost two hundred years ago; you might drive by Deacon Hawley's house, the site of Matthew Seymour's Indian Trading Post, the Episcopal Church, Settlers' Rock, and the red schoolhouse on West Lane, where Eliza went to school.

As for Eliza's red petticoat, that is another story, the one you are about to read. Several accounts of the Battle of Ridgefield mention the red petticoat. I believe the story happened this way. . . .

Chapter 1

Eliza had climbed almost to the top of the giant tulip tree. She was breathless and her long skirts were getting in her way. She was nearly at the place in the top of the huge old tree where she knew she could look out across the countryside for miles and miles around. On a clear spring day like this she and Richard once figured they could see as far as sixty miles away.

She jerked impatiently at her calico skirt and stretched out her foot to reach the next branch. She felt the tree sway with the wind as she went higher and higher, carefully pulling herself up from limb to limb. Her heart pounded with excitement at the thought of what she had come to see.

At last she reached the spot where she knew she could see Long Island Sound. She steadied both feet close together on one limb. Expertly, she wrapped her right arm around the big trunk; then, with her free hand, she pulled an upper branch to one side for a better view through the greenery. Far away, the Sound stretched before her like a strip of the April sky. Beyond the pale water was Long Island, more deeply tinted. Eliza scanned the sheet of water until she spotted what she had come to see. She gasped. There they were—at least twenty or thirty sails huddled together off the Connecticut coast. "The British fleet!" she whispered in awe.

Ever since the Boston Tea Party three years ago the people in towns along the Connecticut coast had lived in terror of invasion by the British fleet. Eliza gazed out across the fourteen miles of rolling fields and woodlands that stretched between Ridgefield, Connecticut, and the Sound. The ships looked like insects creeping over the surface of the water. Eliza thought of the guns and red-coated soldiers the boats carried, and shivered. Then she looked down on the road that twisted, ribbon-like, through the land below her. A man on horseback was moving toward the east, away from Ridgefield.

"Wonder if it's the same man who rode from Norwalk," she mused. "But the man who brought news about the fleet was on a sweated horse, probably couldn't gallop so fast." Eliza had seen the mare being rubbed down outside Squire Keeler's tavern when she hugged Father and Richard good-bye.

She thought about Richard. He had remembered that tomorrow, April 26, was her birthday. She thought about how much she loved her brother, even though he could be so exasperating at times. Only a short time ago he had pinched her elbow and whispered, so Father didn't hear, "I'll think about you on your birthday, Sis."

It was just between the two of them, his being the one to remember, and for a fifteen-year-old brother who delighted in putting toads in an almost thirteen-year-old sister's lunch pail that was pretty good, Eliza thought.

Today she had seen more horses hitched outside Keeler's Tavern than ever before. The men had all looked serious, no one had laughed or smiled. They had talked earnestly in little groups and inspected one another's muskets, while the women looked on with worried expressions.

Eliza loved to go to the tavern. It was on the stagecoach route between New York and Boston and it was a favorite stopping place for travelers. If she were lucky, sometimes she could watch from a polite distance as the travelers climbed out of the stagecoach and went into the tavern through the big front door. Even the door was exciting. It had a huge lion's-head knocker and it was studded to withstand Indian attacks. At least that was what Abigail Bradley had said at school, even though, as Eliza knew, there never had been an Indian attack in Ridgefield. Richard said there was a hidden staircase from the bar up to the ballroom. Since Eliza was always inclined to use her imagination, she had taken this bit of information and made up long, thrilling stories about the staircase.

Keeler's Tavern was the place the men went to for news ever since the Revolution began, especially since the British had taken Long Island. Eliza thought about these things as she watched the horse and rider on the road beneath her grow smaller and smaller, until they looked to her like a tiny black dot on a silver hair.

Impetuously, she took a deep breath and with all her might she shouted, "The British are commmminggg!" The instant her words melted into the air, she was answered with a long low musical sound, like a horn, from the valley behind her. Eliza grinned and swung around to face the northwest. Now, only a few miles away, she saw the undulating ridge of hills called West Mountain. From her high vantage point Eliza felt as though she owned the whole world. Ridgefield lay at her feet, a toy town from her crow's-nest perch. Besides Keeler's Tavern, she

could make out the village green, Matthew Seymour's Indian Trading Post . . . and there, rising up out of the treetops, was the white steeple of the Congregational Church. Eliza squinted. Farther north, Lake Mamanasco looked like a silvery fish laid on its side.

In another moment more horn-like sounds were echoing through the town, farm to farm, across the valley and up the ridge. Eliza knew the music; mothers and daughters all over town were standing in kitchen doorways blowing into conch shells, summoning the menfolk to noontime dinner. Father called them "Kitchen Tritons."

But who in the world is left? Eliza thought as the trumpeting died away. Some of the men had come back from the war to plant the spring crops, but today they were going away again.

Eliza swung around to take one last look at the boats

on the Sound before she scrambled down the tree and started toward home. Home was on West Lane in the southern part of town. Eliza ran down the lane, skirts billowing in the breeze, until she saw her house through the trees. Then she slowed down to a walk.

The house was the dun color that pine boards and chestnut turn when they are never painted. The Bouton home was surrounded by forty acres of land. The Boutons had four cows, two horses, some two dozen sheep, nobody was sure exactly how many, and a stock of poultry, including countless noisy geese.

In front of the house Richard had neatly stacked a woodpile so high that Eliza could barely touch the top of it. To the rear of the house, the rich brown earth had been turned for the spring garden. Later in the summer, squashes would blossom and cucumber vines would trail over the back door. There would be onions, beets, parsnips, currants, tansy for bitters, horseradish for seasoning, and fennel.

There was an ample barn, a bountiful orchard, and a field of clover that was the paradise of bees and birds. And beyond the garden, the barn, and the field was the woods, where the pine and chestnut trees grew. It was from the trees in this forest that the house was built. Everything the Boutons had came from the land—the cherry table and the chestnut cupboard in the kitchen were fashioned by Deacon Hawley from the wood of the trees. The feathers in the soft pillows on the beds had been plucked from the geese, and the snow-white linen sheets had been woven from flax grown in the fields. The fields were divided by rude stone walls, clearing space for cultivation.

Beneath the house was a stone cellar, dark and cool as a cave, lined with barrels of beef, pork, and cider. To Eliza, the barrels always seemed to be fat, little potbellied soldiers lined up for a parade. And they were flanked by sturdy bins of potatoes, carrots, beets, and cabbages.

The garret was more festive. Strings of dried pumpkins, peaches, and apples crisscrossed like party decorations from one side of the room to another. Sweet-smelling bunches of savory, boneset, fennel, and other herbs dangled on strings from the rafters. On the floor were great heaps of wool, piles of flax, and tow.

This was Eliza's world in the year 1777.

As she approached the house, she lifted up her skirts and began to run. She was breathless when she threw open the back door to the kitchen. Her mother was bending over the fire in the huge stone fireplace, stirring a pot of delicious-smelling venison stew.

"Mother!" Eliza's voice was urgent. "I saw the British fleet!"

Mrs. Bouton straightened her back and turned to look into Eliza's face. "You're certain?" she asked.

"Yes!" Eliza almost hissed the words. Her eyes danced with excitement. "There must have been twenty or thirty sails. I climbed our tulip tree!"

She stopped abruptly. Mother never approved of Eliza's tree climbing, especially to such dizzying heights. It wasn't proper for a young lady, she always said.

"Well?" Mother prompted.

"Oh," Eliza said, "I'm sorry. I did climb the tree!"

"Eliza!" Mrs. Bouton exclaimed. "Please, go on!"

"I got to the top, where Richard and I go sometimes, and when I looked toward Norwalk, I saw the sails! I've never seen so many ships on the Sound! They were moving over the water, headed for shore, like a big flock of birds!"

She stopped and stared at her mother, who had gone directly to the corner cupboard and, like a person "possessed," was taking things from it as fast as she could.

"Mother!" she protested.

Her mother's voice was emotionless. "I knew the British were coming, but somehow I couldn't believe it was really so—not until now."

She looked at Eliza over her shoulder. "Hurry," she commanded. "We'll have to hide some of our things." She paused, thoughtfully, then said in a softer voice, "You are old enough to know the danger, Eliza. If the British come to Ridgefield, they will steal or burn everything they see."

She paused, then added grimly, "And I suppose they could get this far by morning."

Eliza was stunned. She hadn't thought of this horrible possibility. She hadn't dreamed that the Redcoats could or would come to their house on West Lane. Her imagination raced on. Come in *our* kitchen, set a torch to *our* house, rummage through our belongings, even our sacred Bible! she thought.

"No wonder the men looked so serious this morning at the tavern," Eliza said aloud.

Mother was kneeling on the floor now, staring at the little assortment of their dearest possessions. The huge family Bible lay on her lap, and strewn around her were Grandmother Hoyt's gold brooch that came from England, the pine box that held the few shillings and pound notes the Boutons possessed, the pewter mugs and plates, and a sampler Eliza had just finished that said "God Bless Our Home." Bordering the words, Eliza had stitched the outlines of their house, the apple trees, and some of the animals.

"Now, what to do with these things?" Mrs. Bouton reflected.

"I'll get a tow sack," Eliza volunteered. And in a few moments she was back from the cellar. Eliza held the sack as her mother gently laid the precious objects inside.

"We could bury it," Mother said, "but the Bible mustn't get wet."

"The basement?" Eliza asked.

"Hmmmmm, no," Mrs. Bouton answered thoughtfully. "The British might burn the house."

"The barn?" Eliza suggested hopefully.

"No, my dear, they will burn the barn, too if they've a mind to."

"I know!" Eliza said. "We won't have to bury it any-place. We can hide it in the root cellar!"

The root cellar was the perfect place. Eliza wondered why they hadn't thought of it first. No one would see the root cellar unless they knew already that it was there. It was built into a little hill where violets grew every spring, and if you didn't go around to the far side of it, away from the house, you wouldn't even suspect it existed. Inside, it was a great vault of fieldstones, damp and cold, and so dark you could barely see into the blackness without a lantern. The same spring that gave the Boutons water in the spring room inside the house trickled in front of the cellar, near the entrance.

Eliza led the way, carrying a lantern. Mother followed her, the bag of precious keepsakes cuddled in her arms as though it were an ungainly baby. The light from Eliza's lantern illuminated a dark corner of the cavernous cellar. Here they hid the bag of valuables, covering it with an empty barrel. They hoped the barrel would protect the Bible from the dampness, for on the pages in the back of the holy book were all of the family records—four genera-tions had chronicled births and deaths and house raisings in this ponderous volume. Eliza loved to pore over these pages of the Bible. Sometimes, after she had studied the entries about the crops, the tree plantings, and the house raisings, she didn't even mind cross-stitching "God Bless Our Home" on the sampler.

She gazed at her mother's shadowy form. "Now," she said softly, "perhaps we will have something else to write in our Bible. . . ."

"Yes, Eliza," her mother answered in a choked voice. "Perhaps we shall."

Chapter 2

Happy birthday, my dear!" Mother said, bending to kiss Eliza on the cheek. Eliza raised her eyes from the dish of applesauce before her and forced herself to smile. Outside, the early morning sun was shining brightly. On any other Saturday morning in spring, and especially on her birthday, Eliza would have been bursting with happiness, full of energy and chatter, but today her heart felt cold and heavy. Listlessly, she stirred the applesauce with her spoon, thinking that to eat now was nothing but a terrible ordeal.

She thought about being thirteen. "April 26, 1777," she said aloud and sighed. She remembered when she was eleven and Father had told Richard about Paul Revere and the Battle of Lexington. And when she turned twelve Father had said it would be a long war. Now, she thought, I'm thirteen and Father and Richard have gone away with the other militiamen from Ridgefield to meet the British.

"Eliza, you haven't eaten a morsel of your breakfast," Mother chided affectionately. Eliza nodded and swallowed the lump in her throat. She wondered if the British would burn rebels' houses if they came through Ridgefield.

"Never mind, child," said Mother, "run along, but try to drink your milk first. You'll need your strength to do Richard's chores."

Eliza ducked her chin, squeezed back her tears, and drank down the milk in three big gulps. It tasted as bitter as a cup of the spring tonic Mother prescribed when anyone looked peaked.

Eliza liked Richard's chores on a Saturday morning better than her own. She liked milking Bessie, collecting the eggs, and pulling down the sweet-smelling hay for the animals. The barn was her favorite place on the farm. She liked to water the horses and curry their sleek backs. Melody and Brownie were gentle horses and it seemed as though they loved Eliza as much as she loved them. Now Eliza was glad to be out of doors in the sunshine. She meandered down the path and opened the gate into the barnyard.

"Happy birthday!" a high, sweet voice called out. Eliza jumped, startled, and turned around.

Abigail Bradley was coming down the lane. Abigail was either Eliza's best friend or her worst enemy. Sometimes Eliza couldn't decide which. The girls were the same age and they shared the *Dilworth Speller* at school.

"If you cannot say something kind about a person, you mustn't say anything at all." Mother's words.

But Eliza couldn't help how she felt sometimes. Abigail was so grown up. She had long black hair, dark brown eyes, and olive skin that never freckled, and she even liked cross-stitching. Eliza was fair, and she hated needlework. Abigail was tall. Eliza was tiny, at least for thirteen.

Abigail tripped daintily up to the fence and gave Eliza a kiss on her cheek. Eliza blushed, but she was glad to receive the affection. "Happy birthday," Abigail repeated.

"Thank you, Abigail." Eliza kicked a stone with her sturdy boot. Then Abigail pulled a small package from her apron pocket and thrust it into Eliza's hands.

"It's for your birthday," she said smiling sweetly. "Hurry, open it!"

Eliza was touched. Abigail was always thoughtful, and somehow, Eliza mused ruefully, she managed to do what was just right. All thumbs, Eliza undid the package. The gift was a pretty linen kerchief, hemmed very neatly, with her name, "Elizabeth," cross-stitched in blue in one corner.

Eliza smiled and her face flushed. "Thank you, Abby, thank you very much. It's beautiful."

Abigail was tapping her foot and looking toward the fields. "I guess your father's gone now too," she said, ready to change the subject.

"Yes," said Eliza softly.

"Have you heard any news?" Abigail sounded anxious.

"No, do you think we shall today?" Eliza asked.

"Well," Abigail said mysteriously, lowering her voice as though she were going to divulge a secret, "I heard Mother tell Father when he left just a few minutes ago that she would have to take us away if worse came to worst!" She paused. "Can you *imagine?* Where would we go? I'm as scared as a jackrabbit, Eliza." She stopped, then added vehemently, "I *hate* Tories!"

Eliza, glad for once to be more virtuous than Abigail, said, "My father says you shouldn't hate Tories. Master Stebbins is a Tory. Father says that they just think differently and sometimes it takes more courage to say what you believe when most folks believe the opposite."

"Maybe." Abigail didn't sound convinced and she tapped her foot again. "Anyhow, they're our enemies now. And they can be spies!" Her brown eyes opened wide.

"Richard went with Father," Eliza interjected. She watched Abigail's face closely.

Abigail's cheeks turned crimson, but she managed to remark carelessly, "Where do you suppose they are right now?" Then, without waiting for an answer, she went on, "Mother said the militia planned to meet General Silliman somewhere between here and the sound."

"We'll just have to wait." Eliza tried to appear resigned. "But, Abby," she said implusively, "I just *hate* waiting!"

"Oh deary me. That reminds me, Mother told me not to stay. I promised her I would come right back," Abigail said. "She'll be as worried as an old hen if I don't get right home. She said to tell your mother that the two of you could come to our house if you like. She said maybe you would feel better if you were with someone else. We womenfolk have to stick together!"

"Thanks, Abby, I'll tell Mother, but maybe everything will be all right." Eliza's heart sank at the very mention of leaving their farm.

After Abigail had disappeared down the lane Eliza stood for a time examining her gift. Every stitch is perfect, she thought wistfully. Then she folded the kerchief neatly, tucked it in her skirt pocket, and resolved to try ever so hard not to disappoint Mother again by complaining when she had to do the needlework or help with the mending.

She liked to climb trees, ride horses, and help with the haying in the fields. But Father said girls were supposed to be gentle and to learn woman's work. "After all," he said, "a woman's work is noble. A young lady must learn to do the things that boys could never do, like sew and mend and cook and spin. Above all," he said, "you must learn patience." Still, Eliza couldn't help but think that boys had more fun.

Worse yet, however, Eliza liked to spend hours resting in the branches of the apple tree or curled up in the hayloft, just dreaming. Sometimes she made up stories and imagined exciting adventures.

Now she ambled toward the barn. Bessie was mooing to be milked and let out into the field. Brownie and Melody whinnied when she opened the gates to their stalls. She pulled apart a prickly hay bale for them, collected the eggs from the hens' nests, amidst loud squawking and flapping of wings, carried two buckets of water from the spring, and checked on the three other cows in the pasture. Each had a new baby calf. Then she stopped in the orchard to gaze at the apple trees, all misty pink with blossoms. She watched a mourning dove fly out of the blossoms and light on a mound of freshly plowed earth.

Eliza could not shake off the awful feeling of loneliness. She missed the sound of Richard's axe ringing against a tree stump. Once she imagined she heard Father's voice, talking to the horses from behind his plow in the back field. But when she paused to listen, everything was quiet. Even the noisy geese that usually waddled around making loud, demanding noises were nowhere to be seen.

The day went by at a snail's pace. She pleaded with Mother to let her go to Keeler's Tavern for news, but Mother wouldn't hear of such a thing.

"You must be patient, Eliza," she said. "We will hear when it is time."

So Eliza finally curled up in the hayloft and thought about the war. She tried to imagine Redcoats landing on the beach at Norwalk, but since she had never even seen a British soldier that was hard to do.

If only I could *do* something, she thought crossly. "Patience *must* be a virtue," she cried aloud, "because it is so hard to be patient!"

She felt even more lonely when she sat down to supper.

She heard her mother's voice but not the words when she said grace. She bit into a slice of rye bread, covered with sweet butter, but a big lump was lodged in her throat and she could barely swallow. The bread and butter tasted bitter. She swallowed hard, but two tears trickled down her pale cheeks.

"Oh, Mother," she finally implored, "will we have to leave the farm and go away somewhere if the British come?" It was a question she had been afraid to ask.

Mrs. Bouton put her hand on Eliza's arm. "You must trust in God, my dear," she said softly.

"But Abigail said Mrs. Bradley might take her away someplace if worse came to worst!" she blurted out.

"Elizabeth Bouton," Mother said firmly, "I want you to put such notions right out of your head. You mustn't go looking for trouble. If trouble finds us we will do what is best.

"But now," she added emphatically, "it is my only daughter's thirteenth birthday, and I haven't given her a gift!" Abruptly, Mother pushed her chair back and went to the corner cupboard. She rummaged around on the top shelf and brought back her sewing box, which she placed in front of Eliza.

"Open your gift, my dear," she said, "and may God bless you on your birthday."

Eliza's blue eyes grew wide with anticipation and her slender fingers trembled as she gingerly lifted the top of the box. The box was filled with beautiful crimson cloth. Slowly, Eliza, drew the contents from the box to unfold the red material. She held it high. It was a red petticoat, ruffled and embroidered at the hem. It was the brightest, fanciest thing she had ever seen. And for some reason, unknown even to Eliza, she threw her arms around her

mother's waist, buried her face in her mother's apron front and sobbed. She clung to the soft, comforting form and wept.

"My petticoat is beautifulllllll!" she wailed. Then she stopped crying, wiped her cheeks with the back of her hand, and smiled. "Thank you, Mother," she said, "I didn't mean to act like a baby."

"Well, I do believe you are too young to cry on your birthday, Elizabeth," Mrs. Bouton teased.

"How did you ever think of it? And you made it without my even knowing?" Eliza said. She glanced toward the chimney corner where the dye tub was kept. Now it was covered with a board and made a cozy seat by the huge fireplace.

"I wanted to make something special. So I thought and thought, until I thought of a red petticoat. I didn't know how to make red dye but I asked around and I found out. I used madder, cochineal, and logwood. Papa bought the cotton in Danbury the day he brought home the West Indies sugar. I dyed it that Saturday you spent the whole day with Abigail and sewed it at night after you were in bed." She paused. "Now, eat your supper and I will tell you a story.

"I remembered this story the day I dyed the cloth, and I said to myself on that day, 'I will tell Elizabeth this story when I give her the petticoat!'"

"Is it about Grandmother Hoyt?" Eliza asked. "And is it a *true* story?"

"As a matter of fact, it is both," Mother answered.

Chapter 3

Eliza was supposed to look exactly like her Grandmother Hoyt, although there wasn't a picture to show the likeness. Eliza, like Grandmother Hoyt, had big blue eyes, taffy-colored hair, and a sprinkling of freckles across the bridge of her nose. So, naturally, Eliza liked nothing better than to curl up in the rocking chair in front of a big fire of sweet-scented hickory on a winter's evening and listen to the stories her mother told about when Grandmother Hoyt was a girl in the Connecticut wilderness.

"Have I heard this story before?" Eliza asked.

"Never," Mother answered.

Eliza held the petticoat up to her waist and swirled around the room.

"Eliza, you look like a whirligig! Sit down and try to eat something," Mother scolded.

Eliza plopped down in her chair and arranged the red petticoat on the back of the chair next to her. Carefully, she spread out the ruffle so that she could admire it.

"As you know, your grandmother was only a baby when your great-grandmother and great-grandfather and the other twenty-six families left Norwalk and bought Catawba Town from Chief Catoonah," Mrs. Bouton began.

"For only a hundred pounds sterling," Eliza interjected, for she had heard this part of the story before. In fact, she had even played around "Settlers' Rock" uptown where the deed had been signed with the Indians.

"The settlers had a treaty with the Ramapo Indians," Mother continued, "and the Indians were friendly and lived up to their contract. But years later—your grandmother was even younger than you are now—two of the tribe came back to Lake Mamanasco to camp and hunt."

Eliza wound her foot around the leg of her chair and sat up straighter. Indians fascinated her.

"It was early spring, just about this time of the year, and none of the townspeople paid them any mind." Mother's voice grew louder. "But one afternoon two Indians appeared in the doorway of this house."

Eliza looked at the kitchen door, imagining the Indians standing there with tomahawks raised aloft.

"Your grandmother was standing right here in the kitchen. She had just filled a pitcher with water, and she was so startled when she looked up and saw the Indians that she dropped the pitcher. Water splashed all over the floor and on her shoes."

Eliza propped her elbows on the table and rested her chin in her cupped hands. The story was beginning to be exciting.

"When the pitcher hit the floor, the crash was like a signal to the Indians," Mother continued. "They let out a big war whoop and leaped into the house. They were looking for something—guns, rum, or maybe food. Grandmother said they started rummaging in the cupboards, opening doors and pulling things off the shelves. Mugs and plates and pots and pans came crashing down. Grandmother said she was frightened speechless. One of the

Indians found an apple pie and picked up the whole pie and started to eat it."

Eliza grinned.

"The other Indian disappeared into the next room," Mother went on, "and luckily for Grandmother, the second followed. Grandmother said she came to her senses enough to know she had better get out of the house just as fast as she could, so out the doorway she sailed!

"Just at that moment an extraordinary thing happened— a miraculous thought entered Grandmother's head! She stopped in her tracks just long enough to reach down and pull off her underskirt. Then she raced as fast as ever her legs would carry her toward the back field, frantically waving the petticoat over her head."

Eliza could not contain herself. "Whatever for?" she cried.

"Well, my dear, it was perfectly sensible, and if you will just be patient a moment I shall tell you," said Mother.

"Her father—your great-grandfather—was cutting timber at the edge of the field and Grandmother knew that if she screamed he might not hear her, but the Indians most probably would. Of course your grandmother knew that an excited Indian is most unpredictable. But, just as she had hoped, her father saw her running out across the field as fast as a runaway horse, her petticoat streaming over her head like a flag, and he knew something must be wrong!

"The Indians came out of the house a moment later. When they saw Grandmother Hoyt, they yowled like wolves baying at the moon and streaked across the field after her, swinging their tomahawks in the air. Fortunately for your grandmother, her father had his musket with him. The Indians had nearly caught up to her when a musket shot rang out across the field and whistled through the air overhead. Your grandmother kept running, but the Indians stopped still for one second before they let out another whoop, turned around, and ran back toward the road, hollering all the way."

Eliza took a deep breath.

"And," her mother concluded, "they disappeared down West Lane."

"Did anyone ever see them in town?" Eliza was curious about the Indians.

"I don't think they were ever seen again in Ridgefield," Mrs. Bouton answered.

Eliza stared dreamily into the fire. Then she reached out and picked up her own petticoat from the back of the chair.

Chapter 4

The big comfortable kitchen had grown darker. The soft breeze that was drifting in the windows so gently when Mother began her story now blew damp and chill. It whipped the tiny flames in the fireplace and the fire sparkled brightly. Eliza gazed out the window and thought it was too early in the evening to be so dark. Then she watched as the sun came out from behind a black cloud. For a moment the room was bathed in a rich golden light. Then the sun disappeared again behind another cloud and the room was filled with dark shadows. She watched the bushes in the yard begin to sway and bow before the ever-increasing wind, as more huge black clouds raced across the sky.

Mother sighed. "I do believe a bad storm is brewing," she murmured.

They stood together at the window for a few minutes, watching the gathering storm in silence. Eliza was thinking about Father and Richard, wondering when there would be news from the Ridgefield militiamen.

The cold wind gathered strength and Eliza knew that soon a downpour would begin. She was about to speak when she felt her mother's hand clutch her arm.

"Listen!" Mother commanded in a whisper.

There was a flash of lightning, followed by a crack of

thunder, but Eliza remained motionless, straining to hear yet another sound. Then she heard it—without a doubt, it was the sound of a horse galloping up the lane!

Eliza and Mrs. Bouton ran out the kitchen door into the blustering wind. A man on horseback was approaching the house. The horse was bucking the wind, the rider was bareheaded and his coattails were flying out behind him.

"It's Squire Keeler!" Eliza cried.

The rider waved and shouted over the pounding hoof-beats, "The British!" His voice split the air. "The British are in Danbury!"

Eliza's heart sank. Danbury was only ten miles north of Ridgefield.

Squire Keeler pulled in the reins as he came abreast of them. The horse reared and halted suddenly. The old man bounded from the saddle. His white hair was churned by the wind and he was breathing heavily.

"The Patriots are on the trail of the Redcoats!" he said loudly. "Our Ridgefield men were with General Silliman at Redding earlier today." He took a deep breath. "But the British are sacking Danbury!"

Her mother gasped. Even Eliza knew that supplies for the Continental troops were stored in Danbury.

Squire Keeler shouted over another sudden gust of wind. "We think there are more than two thousand British foot soldiers, with cavalry and artillery! They landed at Compo Beach late yesterday!"

Horses too! Eliza thought. She hadn't imagined horses on those ships.

"What I'm trying to say, Ma'am, is, I've come to warn you—the British could come through Ridgefield on their way back to Long Island Sound!"

Eliza grasped her mother's hand. Cold drops of rain

began to fall and the strong wind tugged at her long skirt.

"I'm warning all the womenfolk," Squire Keeler bawled over a sudden crack of thunder. "Some are taking the children back into the woods. I know it's no night for it, but do you want to join them?"

Mrs. Bouton stood straight and unyielding. "We will stay in our home tonight, Sir, thank you just the same," she said.

The rain began to come down in torrents. Mrs. Bouton, still holding on to Eliza's hand, ran toward the house and motioned to Squire Keeler to follow. He tossed the reins over the hitching post and ran toward the door.

Inside, the kitchen was dark except for the coals glowing brightly in the fireplace. Mother went to the fireplace and lit a long taper, with which, one by one, she touched the candles on the mantle and on the table. Soon the room was bathed in candlelight. Squire Keeler stood near the kitchen door. Eliza looked at the old man, slight of frame but straight as a young cornstalk. The candlelight cast long shadows on his wrinkled face. She noticed a strange expression in his eyes.

He looks the way Richard did the day he forgot to close the barn door and had to tell Father that the cows had trampled the corn crop, Eliza thought.

"Was there something else, Sir?" Mrs. Bouton inquired gently.

Squire Keeler cleared his throat.

"Yes?" prompted Mrs. Bouton.

"It is a great deal to ask you, Ma'am, and I don't know in my heart if it is right, but since you do have the biggest root cellar in town . . ." his voice trailed off.

He began again, resolutely, "Mistress Bouton, we have valuable supplies here in Ridgefield—gunpowder, clothing, and some grain. We are storing what we can in the church, but we need a place for what is left."

"I must speak for my husband now," Mrs. Bouton said gently. "And I know that Ebenezer would want the Patriots to store the supplies in our root cellar."

"God bless you!" The nervous innkeeper sounded relieved. "But, I am obliged to tell you, Madam, that if the British find the stores in your root cellar, it will go badly for your home."

Mrs. Bouton nodded. "I know," she answered. "Now, may I give you some rum? I'm afraid you may catch a death of cold."

"No thank you, Ma'am. Some of the men are at the church now. What we can't get stored there we will bring down in wagons later tonight."

Squire Keeler bowed gallantly. "Thank you, dear lady, and good night!"

Without waiting for a reply, the old man left. A minute later Eliza heard his horse galloping back down the lane.

Chapter 5

The rain fell in torrents. It splashed at the windows and pattered on the shingled roof. The wind whistled in the chimney and rattled the door. Eliza was glad she had tended the livestock early. Bessie was milked and locked securely in the barn. Melody and Brownie were safe in their stalls, the eggs were collected, and, thought Eliza, those jabbering, loud, arguing geese can very well look out for themselves.

But her thoughts kept darting back to Squire Keeler and the root celler as she readied the tub for her Sabbath bath. Saturday-night baths were a ritual in the Bouton household, as in all the farm homes in Ridgefield.

She laid two pieces of splintered pine on the fire and thought with dismay, Gunpowder in the root cellar! But then that was no stranger than gunpowder in a church. Stoves and fireplaces were not even allowed in the church.

She lugged two buckets of water from the spring room and half filled the cedar tub in front of the fireplace. By that time the kettle of water, hung on a crane over the crackling fire, was steaming; she added that to the tub too. After her bath, she put on her nightdress and combed her long hair. Then she knelt down by her mother in front of the fire and said her prayers.

Eliza had been taught to fear God, never to waste time

or goods, to behave wisely, and to work diligently. To do all of these things was very difficult sometimes, and often she and Richard needed a reminder.

"A good man," her father had told Richard over and over again, "is thrifty, pious, prudent, and progressive."

Every Sabbath the Boutons rode their horses to the Congregational Church, Eliza seated on a pillion behind Richard, Mother behind Father.

Tomorrow would be the first Sabbath in her entire thirteen years on earth that Eliza had not been in church. She had been baptized in the church the first Sunday after she was born, according to the custom.

After her prayers, Eliza rested her head in her mother's lap and watched a hickory log sparkle and smoke. She wondered when the men would come with the supplies.

What do people do when their homes are burned? she asked herself.

Once she thought she heard a low booming noise in the distance that she imagined was cannon fire.

She listened to the raindrops hit the windowpanes and wondered if it could be raining so hard in Danbury. She closed her eyes, and her thoughts went back again to Papa and Richard and the other militiamen. Will they be able to get to Danbury in time to save the town? . . . Redcoats! . . . Maybe I can wear my red petticoat tomorrow . . . How can they fight in the rain? . . . Roads must be knee-deep in mud . . . The thoughts swirled around in Eliza's weary mind until she fell sound asleep with her head resting on her mother's lap.

The next thing she knew Mother was leading her up the steep narrow stairs to her bed. "I must hold a light for the men, Eliza," she was saying. "They are here with the wagons."

Eliza nodded. She heard men's voices outside as she

nestled her head in the softness of the big feather pillow, pulled the bed sheet up to her nose, and fell into a deep sleep.

In her dreams she saw Richard. He looked frightened. He was shivering and his pants and shirt were soaking wet. She saw British soldiers galloping their horses through the streets of Danbury. They were yelling and carrying blazing torches, which they hurled at the houses.

Then she saw more Redcoats marching in straight columns to the rhythmic beat of drums. Rat-a-tat-tat, rat-a-tat-tat . . . The drums were getting louder. The British were in Ridgefield. They were marching straight across the village green, headed down West Lane, past the school-house, straight toward the Boutons' house. Silver bayonets pointed the way, as the horde of Redcoats came closer and closer, their drums beating louder and louder. They halted in front of the barn. One Redcoat flung a torch. . . .

Eliza awoke with a start and lay very still, listening. Something must have wakened her! She lay rigid, clutching the sheets up around her chin, but her eyes were open wide, searching the room, trying to make out what might be in the darkest corners.

Her heart pounded louder than the drums had in her nightmare. She lay motionless for a few seconds, straining to hear a voice, footsteps in the hall, or horse's hooves pounding down the lane. But in the stillness of the night there was only the soothing sound of rain on the roof.

Eliza sighed with relief and relaxed her grip on the sheet. I'm as skittish as a fawn, she thought.

Then she heard her mother's voice downstairs. Eliza wondered who could be with her mother and what time it was. She slipped down from her big four-posted bed and tiptoed to the head of the stairs. All was quiet. She crept down the stairs, trying not to make a sound. Halfway down, she leaned over so that she could peer into the kitchen. In the firelight she saw her mother's ghost-like form, shrouded in her long nightdress. She was kneeling, like a specter, over some dark object on the floor. Eliza studied the eerie spectacle for a moment. Then she ran down the rest of the stairs.

"Mother!" she whispered, then stopped short. A Patriot soldier lay facedown in a heap on the floor and a trickle of blood was oozing from under his still body.

As if hypnotized, Eliza watched. Her mother slipped her hand under the man's chest, searching for a heartbeat. Mrs. Bouton looked up. "He's breathing!" she said. "Quickly, Eliza, get a coverlid and pillow!"

Eliza flew up the stairs. She snatched the quilt and pillow from her bed and bounded back down the stairs. Together, they doubled the patchwork lengthwise and spread it out on the floor close to the soldier's body. Eliza placed the pillow next to his head and noticed that he was almost as long as her quilt. Downright skinny, too, she thought.

"Kneel next to the quilt," Mother directed, "and when I lift his left side, try to pull him over on his back, gently."

Together, they rolled the soldier over onto the quilt, face up. Disbelief clouded Mrs. Bouton's eyes. "Why, he's only a boy," she said tenderly. Mother-like, she brushed a shock of dark hair from the boy's forehead. His face was pasty white, but fresh red scratches covered one cheek. His eyebrows were jet black, his nose fine and sharp. Eliza thought he must be sixteen. "Maybe about a year older than Richard," she guessed.

His uniform was streaked with dirt and soaking wet. One leg of his breeches was red with fresh blood. Eliza shivered. Mrs. Bouton slipped down onto her knees next to Eliza and put her hand under the young man's head. She lifted his head gently and put a mug of rum to his pale lips, but the brown liquid spilled down the boy's chin and onto his chest. The pungent smell of rum filled the air.

Then the boy's eyelids fluttered and his lips parted. Mrs. Bouton upended the mug in a desperate attempt to get some of the rum down his throat. Then, gently she lowered his head back onto the soft pillow.

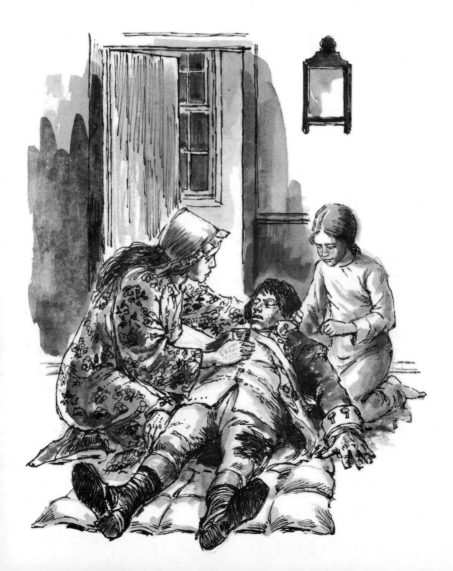

Chapter 6

Eliza and her mother tried to make the young soldier comfortable and to dress his leg wound. Eliza fetched a clean sheet and Mrs. Bouton tore it into strips for bandages. After she pulled off his boots, she cut away the blood-soaked cloth of his breeches leg with sharp shears and swabbed clean the ugly wound with steaming cloths.

Then minutes ticked by. They struggled to remove his wet jacket and pull one of Father's clean, warm nightshirts over his head. Mrs. Bouton and Eliza worked without speaking until they were ready to drag the quilt with its heavy load across the floor into the warmth and light of the fire. Mrs. Bouton studied his drawn face in the firelight and sighed. "He's lost too much blood. If only we could get a doctor!" she said.

But Eliza knew that the nearest doctor was in Danbury, and Danbury was being burned!

The boy breathed heavily, but not once did he open his eyes or move. Eliza noticed that outside the darkness was beginning to fade. The rain had stopped, but the sun was not yet over the horizon.

Mrs. Bouton put her arm around Eliza's shoulders and squeezed. "Watch him closely," she said. "I am going to dress."

Eliza nodded. After her mother had gone she studied the boy's pale, drawn face curiously. It was a handsome face and she was sure she had never seen him in Ridgefield. His skin wasn't so tan as Richard's and his hands were smooth, with long delicate fingers. Probably can't swing an axe, she mused. He sure is a string bean.

Outside the first pale rays of sunlight began to sparkle through the heavy mist that clung to the countryside, as the Sabbath dawn pushed the darkness away from trees, barn, stone walls, and hills. Eliza heard the shrill sound of a bird call. The sky grew lighter, a cock crowed from over the hill, and one of the horses whinnied in the barn. Then the bird solo was accompanied by more trilling and whistling, until the air was filled with music, as though each member of a great chorus was tuning up in a different key, sounding a special melody.

Eliza looked at the big old clock that stood in the corner of the kitchen. It was six o'clock, but Eliza couldn't believe the night had passed so quickly. Now she was bursting with curiosity about the supplies the men had stored in the root cellar.

Finally Mrs. Bouton reappeared, neatly dressed in her best Sabbath calico, with a freshly ironed muslin kerchief precisely knotted around her shoulders, her hair brushed to a high luster.

Eliza took her red petticoat from the chair where she had left it the night before and bounded upstairs. She fumbled with the long row of little buttons up the back of her dress, stuffed her feet into her shoes over twisted stockings, and drew a comb frantically through her hair. Then she lifted her skirt just high enough to see the red flounce on her new petticoat. After a moment of admiration, she raced back down the stairs.

Mother was kneeling on the floor next to the boy. He was gasping for breath, as though he had just pulled his head out of a bucket of water. His eyes opened. He blinked and tried to sit up, but his face contorted with pain and he fell back helplessly onto the pillow.

"You mustn't try to move," Mrs. Bouton said softly.

He sighed heavily and stared at her, bewildered. Mrs. Bouton tried to answer his unasked questions. "You pounded on our door early this morning, just a few hours ago," she said. "When I opened the door, you just fell in!" She paused, then added, "You said you had to see Hawley. You said you had a message."

"I remember." He sighed again, but before he could go on his eyes closed and his head fell to the side; he was unconscious again, back in the strange, dark dreamland from which he had just emerged. Eliza adjusted the pillow so that he could rest more comfortably.

The minutes ticked away slowly on the grandfather clock. The boy slept on until Mother woke him to feed him spoonfuls of warm beef broth. He took the soup like a dutiful child, then sank back into a deep sleep. Once he moaned aloud and writhed in his sleep as though he were trying to wrench himself loose from some invisible bond.

Eliza was impatient to find out where this mysterious figure had come from and who he was. She was certain that he had something to tell them, but she did not have to be told by her mother that he was too sick to be asked questions. Persistently, her thoughts raced from Father and Richard back to the root cellar and the strange young soldier.

She almost jumped with joy when Mother suggested that she go out and do the chores. Richard usually tended the livestock on the Sabbath, the one day of rest, when no real work was allowed. Once she reached the out of doors she felt better. The air was heavy and a fine mist hung over the land. She looked up, squinting into the glare. Overhead gray clouds sailed through the sky, casting shadows on the hillsides from time to time.

"Doesn't feel like Sunday," she said to herself. Then, impetuously, she raced pell-mell to the barn. "First things first," she cried as she shooed Bessie out to pasture and hastily collected two buckets for watering the horses. She ran to the spring, filled the buckets from the wooden pipe, and carried them back to the barn. She was in such a hurry water sloshed out all over her feet.

Eliza loved the horses most of all. They always whinnied when she went to their stalls and acted as though they were glad to see her. But today she didn't take time to stroke their sleek flanks or let them nuzzle at her skirt pocket for a piece of carrot. Brownie sucked up one bucket of water. Melody stuck her brown muzzle in the pail, and almost tipped it over. Eliza caught it just in time. "You better behave today," she said to the horse. "I have lots of other things to do!"

Now, at last, she was ready to investigate. She had been waiting for her chance to look in the root cellar. Now was the time! She shaded her eyes and studied the lane. No one was in sight. She gazed out across the fields. Only a convoy of blue jays zoomed into view, raucously calling back and forth like a pack of noisy boys just released from school.

"Now!" she said to herself, and bounded off to the root cellar. She bent over, stepped into the entrance, and peered inside. As soon as her eyes had become accustomed to the dark, she made out the contents—barrels, wooden boxes, sacks of grain, some guns, and even a stack of uniforms tied together with a rope—hurriedly packed, helter-skelter, in the cave.

It was too much for Eliza's imagination to resist. She reached out and touched one of the muskets with her fingertips and imagined herself standing outside, in front of the root cellar, aiming the gun at an entire regiment of Redcoats. While she held the Redcoats back, the Patriots attacked them from the rear. A fierce battle had gotten under way in her mind when she caught herself, just as she did at school when Mistress Delight Benedict startled her from a daydream behind the *Dilworth Speller*.

She sighed. "No wonder Papa says I'm full of notions," she said, backing out of the cellar. She looked around until she spotted two big branches that had been broken from a tree by the storm. She dragged the tree limbs from the stone wall where they had fallen and leaned them carelessly against the entrance to the root cellar. She stood back to study the camouflage. Satisfied with her accomplishment, she ran back to the house and quietly slipped into the kitchen.

"I'll watch now, Mother," she said softly. "I tended the animals."

"Good girl," her mother said, sounding relieved. "But, Eliza, I've been thinking, perhaps you shouldn't go outside again, not for a while."

Eliza knew what her mother was thinking—the Redcoats were somewhere in the countryside.

Chapter 7

Eliza sat down in the rocker near the soldier. The strain of waiting was becoming almost unbearable. The clock ticked on and on; the minutes crept by at a snail's pace, until, finally, it was eleven thirty.

Eliza shifted in the rocker for the tenth time. "Will he ever wake up?" she asked herself impatiently. She tried counting the ticks the clock made, but she couldn't keep up with the steady "tick, tick, tick, tick." She picked up the ruffle of her red petticoat and nervously ran the cloth back and forth between her fingers. The minutes dragged on. At last the boy moved. Eliza knelt close to him. His eyes opened and he frowned. "Is your mother here?" he asked anxiously. Eliza nodded and called to her mother.

The boy's eyes followed Mrs. Bouton as she came toward him. "You have to hide me, Ma'am!" He sounded desperate, but his voice was stronger and deeper than the first time he had spoken.

"What time is it?" he asked.

Mrs. Bouton looked up at the clock. "It's noon on the Sabbath, son," she said.

"Good Lord, Ma'am, the British should be in Ridgefield by now! For your sake, take your little girl and go! I'll be all right. Please, go!" he persisted. "If the British come

43

in this house it will be worse for you if I'm here. Please!" he implored. "Are there neighbors down the road?"

Eliza trembled. Mrs. Bouton nodded to the boy and put her hand on Eliza's arm. Her fingers were icy, but her voice was calm. "You must rest," she said, ignoring his warning.

The boy spoke anxiously. "I'm Luke Scott, Ma'am, I'm carrying a message from General Wooster for General Washington. I've got to go on somehow, or find someone to take my letter." He looked at his jacket, hanging on a peg by the fireplace.

He seemed to muster all the strength left in his frail body in order to go on. "Danbury was a sea of fire last night!"

"But the British aren't here yet. We're all right," Mrs. Bouton said. "Now you must rest a bit longer, at least until you get your strength."

Luke Scott looked at her thoughtfully, and then he spoke in even tones, as bit by bit he unwound his tale. He said a sniper had shot and wounded him just a few miles outside of Danbury, then followed him on horseback down the dark road to Ridgefield.

"The roads were muddy and the sniper almost caught up to me," he said. "I jumped from my horse. It was my only chance to escape. It was so dark that the sniper followed my horse just as I had hoped he would. Then I tried to find my way on foot." He stopped, then added, "And here I am in your house. My leg hurt so, Ma'am, I don't remember much after that except how glad I was when I saw the light!"

His story finished, Luke closed his eyes wearily and sank back into a half-conscious state of shock and exhaustion.

Mrs. Bouton took his wrist. Eliza watched silently while her mother felt the boy's pulse.

Gently she rested his arm on the quilt. "I shouldn't have let him talk so long," she reproached herself.

For a moment there was only the sound of the clock ticking loudly. Then the eerie silence was broken by a low, distant boom. Eliza's heart pounded furiously. She stared at her mother in disbelief. It was the unmistakable sound of cannon!

"They're here!" she cried. "The British are here!"

Chapter 8

The distant rumble of cannon fire split the silence again.

"Eliza!" Mrs. Bouton's voice was resolute. "You must go alone! I'll tie some food in a napkin. Go down the cow path to Abigail's. If the Bradleys have fled, hide in the blueberry patch beyond the field. I will come for you when it is safe."

Mrs. Bouton took a napkin from the table and a loaf of bread from the cupboard. Eliza saw her mother's hands tremble, and tears welled up in her own eyes.

She ran to her mother and threw her arms around her, sobbing. "Mother, please!" she beseeched. "Please, I *can't* leave you here, you and him."

Mrs. Bouton stroked her hair. "Eliza," she soothed. "I am trying to do what is best for you." She hesitated, as though she were thinking aloud. "Perhaps the Bradleys could help us move Luke. It's only for a few hours. By tomorrow the British will surely be gone."

"Then please let me go and see if I can get help," Eliza implored. "But I can't run away and hide. I'm sure the cannon are no closer than the village green!"

Mrs. Bouton stared silently at Luke. Eliza knew her mother felt the way she did. To separate in time of danger wasn't right.

46

"We are all responsible, one for the other." Eliza recalled her mother's words to Richard once not so long ago.

Now Mrs. Bouton spoke softly. "My heart has gone out to the boy. It's almost as though *he* were Richard. Both of them—fighting a war! They ought to be farming and learning from books. Just boys. . . ." Her voice trailed off.

Eliza began to think of a plan.

"I won't go to the Bradleys!" she said aloud. "They would have gone by now! I'll head uptown instead. If anyone is moving a wagon out I'll see them on High Ridge Road." Her eyes sparkled with excitement. "And, with a wagon, we could get Luke out in time!"

Eliza knew the narrow cart path would not be taken by the British army. They would march, instead, right down the main road, along the green, past the smithy's and the meetinghouse, then perhaps to Keeler's Tavern— the way the stagecoach went.

"Eliza, you *are* clever!" said Mrs. Bouton.

Eliza's jaw dropped. Compliments were seldom given in the Bouton household and when they were it was seldom Eliza who received them. Since she had the hardest time being patient and mindful, she rarely was so openly praised. Once, sent upstairs to fetch Mother's knitting, Eliza brought back a water pitcher, and another time, sent to gather the eggs, she had stepped on a hen's nest because she had been so intent on examining a spider web.

Now Mother said she was clever!

She put her arms around Mrs. Bouton's neck, hugged her, and ran out. "I'll be back by one!" she called.

She had made this same short journey many a summer morning, running errands for Papa. She would not go any farther than the smithy.

She started up West Lane at a jog, then slowed down to a walk when she reached High Ridge. She would follow High Ridge northward on the west side of the village green. Main Street followed northward on the east side of the green.

The narrow dirt road was still wet from the night's rains. The air was cool and sweet with the fragrance of blossoms on some hidden tree bordering the road. Since it was only April, most of the trees did not yet have all their leaves. The maples were sprinkled with red shoots, and the tall, graceful elms were covered with downy feathers of the palest green. Nothing stirred.

"It's too quiet," Eliza thought.

Then a deep, hollow roar broke the silence. The cannon sounded as though it came from uptown. It could be right on the Danbury Road, Eliza thought.

A squirrel began chattering and fussing in a tree branch high overhead. Eliza looked up and grinned. "Complaining at *that* noise won't do you any good," she said.

She continued up High Ridge at a faster pace. A chipmunk darted across her path and skittered into a secret nook in a stone wall. The walls reached down into the border of woods that separated High Ridge from the pastures beyond. Papa had always said the walls were monuments to the settlers who had wrenched the stones from the earth.

Eliza had a warm feeling of affection for the land. She thought the colony of Connecticut must be the most beautiful place in the whole world. And since she had heard her father read aloud from the family Bible every day of her life, she recalled her favorite passage:

"For, lo, the winter is past, the rain is over and gone; the flowers appear on the earth; the time of the singing of birds is come, and the voice of the turtle is heard in our land."

But so is the rumble of cannon fired by King George's soldiers, she thought anxiously, stopping on the road to listen.

She heard the unmistakable crack of musket fire in the distance. North of town she noticed blue smoke billowing up in great clouds from the direction of Lake Mamanasco. She gazed at the smoke rising above the treetops.

"That's about where Isaac Keeler's gristmill is," she said to herself. "If any folks are heading out of town, surely they would be this far by now!"

She was puzzled. If there is fighting it must be closer to the green, or else I couldn't hear the shots, she thought.

The leaves of the bushes next to the path rustled. Eliza froze. She held her breath, listening. She knew that she was just behind the Congregational Church on Main Street, where Patriots had stored the supplies. She stood, listening, for a few seconds longer, then she relaxed.

I'm as skittish as a scared rabbit, she decided, but I'd better head back home soon.

She felt as though she had failed Luke and Mother. "I guess I dropped my bucket in an empty well," she muttered gloomily.

She wondered what they would do now.

Pray the British don't see our house! she thought.

Then suddenly, there was another crackling in the bushes behind her. Eliza caught her breath sharply and turned around in the path, deliberately continuing back down the trail at a measured gait, listening as she took each step.

A twig snapped in the bushes. She paused. Silence. Then she heard the sound of leaves rustling behind her. Her heart pounded wildly. She picked up her skirts and began to run, as fast as she could, toward home.

Someone was chasing her!

The distinct sound of footsteps thudded behind her at a fast jog but she didn't dare to look.

They're catching up! she thought, trying to run even faster. The footsteps quickened. Panic-stricken, she pushed herself forward with all her might, and kept running.

Suddenly, catching her toe in a tree root, she pitched forward onto the wet ground. The fall knocked her breathless. She lay stretched out in the path, facedown, too terrified to move, and listened to the footsteps approach. She clenched her fists and waited, trembling.

"Well, what in the world!" a scratchy boy's voice rang out.

Eliza pulled herself up off the ground and scrambled to her feet, shaking. She would not have been surprised to see a Redcoat, but instead she looked up into the face of Jeremiah Plunket, the boy who sat in the back row at school. Furious tears flooded her cheeks.

"You nearly frightened me to death!" she cried.

Jeremiah stared at her, bewildered.

"Aren't you glad I'm not a *Redcoat?*" he entreated.

Eliza brushed the twigs and dirt from her damp face and skirt front and nodded absentmindedly.

Of all human beings! she thought resentfully.

Jeremiah was only a year older than Eliza. He was quieter than the other boys at school and stayed to himself. Jeremiah's parents were dead and he lived with his aunt. Eliza had often thought how hard it must be for a boy to get along without a father or a mother.

He was the smartest boy in West Lane School with his sums, but on a horse he looked like a teetering scarecrow. And even though he was one of the biggest boys in town, everybody knew he was so clumsy he was most apt to fall over his own feet. Just last winter he stepped on Mistress Delight Benedict's toe when he went up to recite and she rapped him on the knuckles with her pointer so hard that tears sprang to his eyes.

Eliza had felt sorry for him then, but now she was thinking that the last person in the world she would want to depend on for help was the one standing directly in front of her.

And he's frightened the wits out of me! she thought.

Jeremiah flushed. He shifted his weight from one foot to the other and self-consciously shoved a fist in his breeches pocket.

The momentary, awkward silence was broken by the whine of musket shot and the distant sound of men's voices.

"Eliza," Jeremiah rasped, "there's been a battle by Master Stebbins' house. I have to get you out of here, fast!"

He grabbed Eliza's hand and headed toward West Lane. His long legs took such big strides that Eliza's feet barely touched the ground, as she skipped and ran to keep up. She thought Jeremiah would wrench her arm from its socket if he pulled her along any faster.

At last he slowed down to a walk and relaxed his grip on her hand. Eliza was breathless, but she tried to keep up, running along beside him.

"Jeremiah," she panted, "we have trouble at the farm!"

Jeremiah leaned forward and took longer strides.

"I have to get you back safe to your mama," he declared.

Eliza felt foolish, but she persisted. "We have a

wounded man—I mean boy." She stopped in the path, but Jeremiah continued on ahead of her. She had to run again to catch up.

"Jeremiah!" she called after him. "There's a wounded soldier in *our* house and we can't let the British find him or they'll kill him, or, or . . ."

"Don't worry, Eliza, we'll think of something!" Jeremiah answered. Then half to himself, half to Eliza, he muttered, "If I had my way, I would be a soldier."

He stopped to let Eliza catch up. Then, as they walked along together, Jeremiah began to tell Eliza about the battle. "The British met our men not far from Settlers' Rock. They'll be sending scouts downtown soon, if they haven't already!" His eyes snapped and the words tumbled from his lips.

"Our men built a big barricade right across Main Street, next to Squire Stebbins'. We used carts, logs, and stones. They let me help!" he said with pride.

"But then," he went on bitterly, "they told me to go home. They said I was too young.

"But I didn't go home!" he sounded angry. "I hid in the woods. I watched the whole battle! I saw General Arnold's horse shot from under him. A whole platoon fired on him, but he wasn't touched, only his horse. When he tried to get away from his horse a Tory rushed up with his bayonet, screaming 'You are my prisoner,' but General Arnold hollered right back, 'Not yet, Daddy, one live man is worth ten dead ones!' And he drew his pistol and shot the man!"

Eliza's mouth dropped open. She was dumbfounded. This morning, while I watered the horses, she thought incredulously, Papa and Richard were fighting Tories not more than three miles away!

Chapter 9

Jeremiah and Eliza turned on to West Lane.

"You should have seen the Dragoons!" said Jeremiah.

They quickened their steps, and the faster they walked the faster he spoke. "They were wearing bright yellow breeches and tall hats that bullets couldn't go through—big feathers on top of the hats!"

He stopped and took a breath. "I shouldn't carry on," he said.

Eliza understood. "I think you were brave to stay and watch," she said, but she didn't think she had made Jeremiah feel any better.

They reached the woodpile in front of the house and Jeremiah stopped walking. "The Redcoats have already burned at least three or four houses," he said, glancing at the Boutons' dun-colored saltbox. "I heard our men talking. The British killed all of Tom Mead's cows. Then they filled his well with stones. Mrs. Mead was so riled up that when a Redcoat started in the back window she took to his fingers with her butcher knife!"

Eliza winced. "Maybe," she ventured, "maybe they won't see our house at this end of town." She couldn't bear the thought of having to use a butcher knife on anyone.

"I don't want to frighten you, Eliza, or your mother, but they'll send out scouts and they'll do as much burning as they can along the way. They're headed back to the boats at Compo Beach, and they're roaring drunk!"

The two trudged up the path to the kitchen door. Mrs. Bouton was waiting. She looked worried.

"Jeremiah!" she cried. "Where is your aunt? Is she all right?"

Jeremiah nodded. "She's fine, Ma'am. She went to South Salem yesterday to help Sis." He blushed. "Jessica's having a baby. Matter of fact, I might be an uncle already for all I know.

"Likely Auntie Agnew hasn't heard the news. I plan to head for South Salem soon as I can."

Mrs. Bouton put her hand on Jeremiah's arm and drew him into the house. "We're glad you are with us," she said.

Eliza noticed that Jeremiah was a head taller than her mother. Why, he must be as big as Papa already, she thought. Then, turning toward the figure still lying on the floor, Eliza asked, "How is Luke?"

Mrs. Bouton looked at the thin, quiet figure in Papa's nightshirt and shook her head. "I'm afraid he's worse." She looked at Jeremiah. "Did Eliza tell you?"

"Yes Ma'am," he answered.

"He's lost a lot of blood. He doesn't have the strength in him of a wilted buttercup." She shook her head. "I doubt that he can be moved now, in any event."

Jeremiah cleared his throat. "Mrs. Bouton, Ma'am, you and Eliza take a night's rations and go into the woods. I know you'll be safe away from the house. I'll stay with the soldier."

Mrs. Bouton looked directly at Jeremiah. "Do you know something we don't?" she asked.

54

Jeremiah shuffled his heavy boot on the pine floor beneath it. "I told Eliza, Ma'am. I saw the Redcoats just a while ago. Matter of fact, I hid behind a big rock and watched them come into Ridgefield. There are thousands of them and they had three cannons up in the front. General Arnold was waiting for them right next to Squire Stebbins' house," he went on.

"But they started firing their cannon long before they got there. When they came within musket shot, our men started shooting." Jeremiah's voice cracked like a rusty hinge.

Mrs. Bouton's eyes widened.

The boy resumed his story. "General Arnold's charger was shot right from under him. After it was over I reckon there must have been thirty or forty men lying there at the barricade, wounded or dead."

Eliza saw her mother's face turn ashen.

Jeremiah noticed too. He stopped short and gulped. "Is Mr. Bouton with the militia?" He looked around the room. "And Richard?" he asked.

Mrs. Bouton nodded.

"I'm sorry I spoke up." Jeremiah looked embarrassed. "But I didn't see them when the British charged, Ma'am."

"It's all right, Jeremiah. I wanted to know. I asked you," Mother answered.

"The wounded were mostly Redcoats, Mrs. Bouton. The British were taking them into Squire Stebbins' house. He had a big white cross on the front of his house. He wanted the British to know he was a Tory, I reckon.

"I met a boy there from Danbury. He said all the Tories in Danbury used limestone to cross their houses and that not one with a cross was burned."

"So, the British have some scruples," said Mrs. Bouton bitterly.

"They're heading down Main Street, south," Jeremiah continued. "Eliza and I heard the cannon firing in the direction of Keeler's Tavern. Please, Ma'am, ladies shouldn't be around here now!" His voice cracked. "I'll stay with this soldier and look after him. You can trust me. Please, go!" he urged.

Mrs. Bouton considered what Jeremiah had just told her.

Eliza knew that Jeremiah was right.

If the British find a Patriot soldier here they will take him prisoner and burn our house and barns! she thought.

But if Luke is moved, he'll probably die! The thought of coming back home and finding only a few smoldering sticks was more than Eliza could bear.

Jeremiah was impatient. "Excuse me, Ma'am, but the British might be coming down West Lane any time. Please, go," he implored, "and let me stay."

Mrs. Bouton had made up her mind.

"No, Jeremiah," she said firmly. "You are a good young man and you may be right, but I can't leave my house, or, or . . ." she faltered, "or you and that poor boy lying on the floor!"

She smiled. "You know, Jeremiah, I have always said I was born here and I shan't leave until I am carried out in my coffin. And I don't intend for that to be anytime soon," she added grimly.

Hoyt spirit, thought Eliza.

She knew there was no need to try to coax her mother to change her mind. She was only relieved that nothing more was said about sending her away to hide in the blueberry patch.

Mother thinks the British are too close for that now! she decided.

Chapter 10

Waiting, Eliza decided, is the worst curse one has to endure on this earth! I know just exactly how Jeremiah must feel, not being allowed to fight with the militia! she thought. I would take a gun and fight the British myself, if they would let me!

She clutched the knife more determinedly and sliced through the bread with enough energy to cut a stone. She was reminded of what Jeremiah had told her about Mrs. Mead and the Redcoat who had tried to come in her window. Cold prickles ran down Eliza's spine and she resolved to put the thought from her mind. She stacked the thick crusty pieces of bread on a dish and carried it to the table.

"You need strength in your body in emergencies," Mrs. Bouton had commented earlier. Now she was loading the table with warm applesauce, sliced beef, potatoes, pickles and horseradish, dried peach pie, and mugs of cider. Cooking on the Sabbath was forbidden by the church, so the sumptuous meal was already prepared.

Eliza marveled at her mother's composure as she went about setting the food on the table. Just as though there was no war on our village green, Eliza thought. She noticed, too, the glint of determination in her mother's eyes and remembered what Papa had said about a woman's courage.

"Oh, fiddledeedee," she told herself. "Papa was right. It takes courage to be patient and carry on when everything is out of joint!

"Thank goodness," she went on, "we have Jeremiah." She had already decided that she would have to apologize to Jeremiah for being so cross when he had surprised her in the woods. As it had turned out, Jeremiah was already being a help. It had been his idea to fashion a stretcher from the bean poles in the garden so that Luke could be moved upstairs to a comfortable bed.

Now he was just outside the door, working on the stretcher. He had left the kitchen door open and Eliza could see him kneeling on the ground over his work.

Luke was sleeping fitfully, tossing and turning and crying out from time to time to some imaginary demon in his dreams.

Eliza went to the doorway to watch Jeremiah. His rough hands skillfully knotted the hemp rope to one of the long poles; next, he laid the rope across the ground a short distance to the opposite pole, knotted the rope securely and stretched it back at an angle to the first pole.

She watched the procedure, fascinated. She imagined Luke lying on the stretcher. Then in her mind's eye she pictured his pale form in her father's big bed. Then she imagined she saw a swarm of Redcoats clamoring to be let in the house.

For a few moments she was oblivious of Jeremiah and everything around her. She was thinking of what she might do if the British *did* come!

Her eyes brightened, sparkling mischievously, and she

was just about to speak when Jeremiah drawled, "Well, Eliza, It's all finished." He held the stretcher upright before her.

"You did it so quickly!" she marveled.

Jeremiah leaned the stretcher against the wall just inside the door.

"Here it is," he said proudly.

"Why, it's perfect!" said Mrs. Bouton as she studied the litter and tugged at one of its cross ropes. "And it's sturdy enough to hold an ox, I'll wager!"

Jeremiah grinned.

"But," she went on, "we shan't move Luke until we've eaten."

Jeremiah's eyes brightened when he saw the assortment of foods that had been placed on the table. The three bowed their heads reverently and Jeremiah began, "Bless this house, O Lord, we pray. Make it safe by night and day. And let thy peace reign over us. Forgive us our sins, that we may work to earn our bread, with love in our hearts and souls fulfilled. Amen."

"What a beautiful blessing, Jeremiah," said Mrs. Bouton when he had finished.

The boy fidgeted. "My pa taught it to me before he died," he said.

Mrs. Bouton broke the awkward silence that followed Jeremiah's mention of his father.

"Do you like to read?" she asked gently.

Jeremiah's face lighted up. "Reading and whittling, Ma'am," he said and beamed. "I've read this year's almanac three times, cover to cover. I know *Watts' Psalms and Hymns* by heart, but I just don't have much else to read."

He fumbled in his pocket and pulled out a small wooden

object and set it down on the table in front of Mrs. Bouton's plate. It was an exquisitely fashioned image of a Patriot soldier.

"I just whittled this one. Would you like to have it?" he asked eagerly.

Mrs. Bouton turned the figure around slowly. Then she picked it up gingerly and held it between her thumb and forefinger to examine it closely. The Lilliputian form looked so real to Eliza that she imagined she heard it cry out indignantly to be set back down on its own feet.

"I've never seen anything so finely carved," Mrs. Bouton said admiringly. "Thank you very much!"

Jeremiah beamed at the praise. "I started it a couple of weeks ago," he said, "after Reverend Ingersol said in meeting that our soldiers from Ridgefield were 'no strutting fops, in militia buckram, raw blue and buff, all fuss and feathers.' I liked that. I plan to carve a Dragoon now, if I can remember enough of how they looked." He paused thoughtfully. "But I've never tried to carve a feather. That will be hard."

Eliza wondered how Jeremiah, with his bumbling great hands, could create such a small object as the delicately chiseled soldier. He had even managed to carve wrinkles in the man's breeches, and the wood had been so artfully rubbed and oiled that the soldier's musket reflected the light.

Mrs. Bouton set the figure on the top shelf of the cupboard. From that vantage point, the small erect Patriot surveyed the kitchen as though it were a battlefield stretched out beneath him.

When she returned to the table Mrs. Bouton slipped a small leather-bound book next to Jeremiah's place. A tattered silk ribbon hung from the gilt-edged pages.

62

"This is *Canterbury Tales*, Jeremiah. My mother's mother brought it with her from England, so I can't give it to you, but you may borrow it and read it whenever you like."

The boy's eyes sparkled. "Thank you, Ma'am," he said. Reverently, he took the volume in his big hands to study it as though it were a rare jewel.

Books were precious in the country and in all of Connecticut even a newspaper was a rarity. Once in a great while the Boutons had a paper. Mrs. Bouton would read aloud from it after supper and Eliza, listening, would let her imagination take up the stories where the newspaper left off.

Mrs. Bouton asked Jeremiah if he would like another piece of pie.

Gracious, thought Eliza, it's his third piece.

"I shouldn't eat so much," Jeremiah said, hesitating, before he held up his plate. "But this is the best pie I ever ate!"

"You will need the energy," Mrs. Bouton assured him as she lifted a big piece of peach pie onto his plate.

"Yes'm, I reckon we should be getting that soldier up to bed. I almost forgot where I was for a while." He dug his fork into the pie.

"Mother," Eliza said, "I have a plan, if the British should come here. I thought of it just a little while——" She stopped short.

The crack of musket fire sounded down the lane. The three froze, listening. The distant sound of a man's raucous voice carried into the room. Jeremiah's fork clattered on the floor as he bounded from the table. Eliza and Mrs. Bouton followed him to the front room, where they crowded around the window, straining to see down the lane.

Eliza, peering through the wavy pane of glass, caught a glimpse of red at the far end of the lane. The ripe tomato color was more vivid than anything she had ever seen, even her own birthday petticoat. As she watched, the patch of red separated into two.

Silently, she watched the two blurred red forms come toward the house. As the forms advanced, Eliza could see, without a doubt, the clear outlines of two British soldiers.

She sprang from the window and ran back into the kitchen, followed by Jeremiah and Mrs. Bouton. "I know how we can save Luke!" she cried as she dropped to her knees before the fireplace and scooped up a handful of gray ashes.

"I imagined a story this afternoon while Jeremiah made the stretcher. I thought of how we might save Luke if the British did come!" Her voice was breathless with excitement, and as she spoke she turned to Luke and let the ashes sift between her fingers onto his head. Then she ran her hand back and forth through his brown hair.

Suddenly, the young soldier looked old. His face was white and drawn; his hair, iron gray.

Eliza stood up, pleased with the miracle she had wrought. "In my story," she said excitedly "we told the Redcoats that 'our father' was deathly ill, and they went away and left him unharmed."

Jeremiah and Mrs. Bouton stared at her. Then Jeremiah found his tongue. "You're right," he said, "but we'd better get 'our father' upstairs before they get here! They'll be more apt to believe it's your pa if he's in a bed!"

There was a flurry. Jeremiah grabbed the stretcher and in seconds Mrs. Bouton was helping him load Luke onto it. Eliza grabbed Luke's jacket and boots and started up the stairs.

"Get the gun by the fireplace. We may need it!" she heard her mother say.

"Dear Lord, don't let Jeremiah have to shoot that gun," Eliza prayed silently.

She dropped the jacket and boots on the floor in the bedroom and kicked them under the bed. She heard her mother and Jeremiah laboriously struggling up the narrow stairs with their awkward burden.

Next she thought, The curtains! The room would have to be dark if they were to fool the British soldiers into thinking Luke was Father.

She ran to the window at the front of the house. Her hand clutched the calico curtain. The sound of a man's voice came through the open window.

"The house is right ahead," the rough voice rang out.

He means *our* house! Eliza thought.

Then another crude voice called over the muffled clomp, clomp, clomp of a horse's hooves, "Is it deserted?"

The first voice answered in a loud sneer. "Abandoned, I'll wager. Like rats deserting a sinking ship!"

"Hey, Jones," the second voice called again from farther down the road. "I'm hungry. Ask the lady of the house if dinner is ready. If it ain't, tell her we'll cook the dinner with the house!" He laughed loudly.

Eliza paled and her small body involuntarily trembled with rage and fear. "Jones," she whispered, as she watched the first Redcoat round the end of the woodpile. His left arm hung in a sling.

Then, as the second soldier came into view, Eliza stared in utter disbelief. He walked with great difficulty, his arms wrapped around a large clock that was obviously heavy and unwieldly. As he struggled up the path, the last of the trio appeared—an officer, riding a large chestnut stallion.

65

She pulled back from the window. They were close enough to see her plainly if they should look straight up. She wanted to run and hide under the bed, the way she did when she was a little girl, afraid of thunder and lightning. Beads of sweat covered her forehead, but her hands were ice cold.

"*I have to be brave!*" she told herself. She clenched her fists and thought of Grandmother Hoyt.

Redcoats can't be any worse than excited Indians, she resolved.

At that moment, Eliza did exactly what her Grandmother Hoyt had done in the face of danger more than half a century before—she threw up her calico skirt and

tugged frantically at the petticoat beneath it. An instant later she was waving the petticoat out the window as a signal to the Redcoats below.

"Oh, ho!" bellowed soldier Jones, the first to see the red flag. "Look at what we've routed out! Can it be that red banner is attached to a loyal countryman?"

Eliza knelt at the window, holding her face down out of sight. She gripped the petticoat much as she would have held a stiff paper to fan a fire. Slowly, she raised and lowered her arms and the red petticoat billowed in the breeze.

"I say up there," hollered Jones, "if you be for the King, show your face!"

Eliza raised herself up on her knees and solemnly looked down at the Redcoats. The late afternoon sunlight shone full on her small freckled face as she peered over the bright red cloth.

"Well, bless my soul, this goodwife isn't very old, is she?" he laughed. "Now, dear Goody, where's your man?" Jones was making fun of her.

"My father's here in his bed, at death's door, Sir. My mother's by his side," she faltered, glancing over her shoulder at Mrs. Bouton and Jeremiah, who stood side by side, staring at her from the shadowy recess of the room. She saw dismay on her mother's face and disbelief in Jeremiah's eyes. Luke was safe in bed.

"My father is dying," Eliza went on in a quavering voice that carried clearly out the window to the trio of soldiers below. The three upturned faces stared at her. Jones swaggered over to the woodpile, dropped his musket on the ground and sat down next to it, cross-legged, resting his back against the wood.

He peered up at the officer on horseback. "Why don't I go in and have a look around, Lieutenant, Sir?" he asked.

Eliza looked at the officer. His face was creased with a network of fine lines, but it was a handsome face, Eliza thought. His uniform wasn't as rumpled and dirty as his foot soldiers' and instead of a musket and bayonet, he wore a saber at his side.

"No," the lieutenant answered Jones wearily.

Eliza sighed with relief.

"I've seen enough death for one day," the lieutenant went on. "I've no stomach for watching this little girl's father die in his bed."

I hope I am forgiven for telling a lie, Eliza thought.

"But, Sir," Jones wheedled, "suppose our pretty miss up there is lying? How do we know she has a sick father 'at death's door'?" He mimicked Eliza's voice.

Her lips trembled and her face flushed with anger. She saw the swarthy soldier, who had been preoccupied with the clock, lug his precious timepiece to the woodpile and carefully balance it on top before he flopped down next to Jones, ready for a rest and more sport with Eliza.

She studied the clock and thought she recognized it. Yes, she did. It was one of the few imported treasures in Ridgefield and it belonged to the Goodspeeds uptown.

These soldiers must have been to the Goodspeeds! Suppose they've burned their house! The thoughts streaked through her mind. If only they won't come in! She wished with all her heart that she could say or do something to make them go on.

Suddenly the officer swung down from his mount. "There will be no more 'cat and mouse' with the little girl!" he warned his soldiers.

"They *are* coming in!" Eliza's heart sank to the pit of her stomach. Her throat felt dry.

"I'll take a look in the house," the officer was saying. "Jones, you and Scraggs look around the barn," he commanded. "And leave the animals alone," he snapped. "We don't need a cow. If you're hungry, I'll take hung beef from the cellar."

Cellar, Eliza echoed the word in her mind. Suppose Scraggs and Jones discover the root cellar! She pulled in her red flag and drew back into the room. Her clenched fists relaxed their grip and her birthday present fell in a heap on the floor beneath the window. Her shoulders drooped.

Jeremiah and Mother were bending over Luke. They had drawn the curtains on the other window and the room was almost dark. Luke moaned. Mother lifted the bandage from his leg and pressed fresh linen strips on the wound. The trip upstairs had not been good for Luke. His wound was bleeding again.

"The officer is coming to search!" Eliza whispered. "I'll go let him in."

"Keep him downstairs as long as you can!" Jeremiah rasped as he shoved a heap of blood-soaked bandages under the bed. He was on his hands and knees wiping up the drops of blood that made a telltale path from the top of the stairs to the bed when Eliza ran out of the room.

There was a loud banging on the front door. The lieutenant was pounding at the locked door with the hilt of his sword. Eliza lifted the lock and flung open the door. The expression on the lieutenant's face told her that he found his job distasteful.

His back was as straight as a ramrod; he had a fair complexion, wispy blond hair, and piercing blue eyes.

Without replacing the sword in its scabbard, he strode past Eliza and went directly into the kitchen. His eyes darted over the room. Then he turned to Eliza. "Now, young lady, where is your ailing father?" he asked.

"He's upstairs," Eliza whispered. She was too terrified to speak aloud. She nodded toward the stairs as a sign to the Redcoat officer that this was the way.

Then she remembered that she should give Jeremiah and Mother more time with Luke. "Would you like to see our cellar first?" she asked timidly.

The lieutenant frowned at her curiously. It sounded as though she were inviting him to have a cup of tea or ad-mire a beautiful view. He shook his head and muttered an oath to himself.

Eliza followed close behind as he headed up the stairs. Halfway up he turned around abruptly. Eliza started. "You're like a puppy dog at my heels," he commented wryly. Eliza was in a trance. She stared, unblinking, at the end of his nose.

"What a strange child," he grumbled.

At the top of the stairs he turned toward Eliza for a signal. She nodded and pointed toward the door to her own room.

"This will give Jeremiah and Mother a few more seconds!" she congratulated herself.

The lieutenant pushed open the door to her room and respectfully walked in. He saw the neatly made bed and wheeled around. "I wanted to see your *father!*" he sputtered, annoyed and exasperated.

"Oh!" Eliza sounded surprised, but now she looked at the door to her father's room and nodded.

With the determined gait of an impatient man who at last has cornered his quarry, the lieutenant abandoned his gentle manner. He brought the heels of his riding boots down hard on the bare pine floor, flung open the door without any pretense of reverence for the dying, and strode across the room.

Jeremiah had completely disappeared! Mrs. Bouton was bending over Luke. Trying to shield his face, Eliza thought.

She watched the lieutenant's eyes as they searched the room. They traveled from the plain whitewashed walls to the curtained window, down to the wide pine boards on the floor, then over to one of Luke's dusty shoes that was only half under the bed! It was too small to be her father's boot.

Eliza's instinct was to cry out, but she held her breath as the lieutenant reached out for the shoe with his sword tip and flipped it out in front of him.

"Whose shoe?" he demanded.

Eliza heard her own voice, as though it came from somewhere else in the room. "It's my brother's shoe, Sir," she faltered. "He's, he's gone to try to find the preacher."

The lieutenant looked at her closely. "Humph!" he grunted.

Luke groaned and coughed. He was coughing blood! Eliza saw her mother hover over him, wiping the blood from his pale lips.

The officer was taken aback. "What's the matter with your husband, woman?" he asked gruffly, peering over Mrs. Bouton's shoulder, trying to see into the face of the figure on the bed.

Mrs. Bouton looked up for a moment, then turned back to Luke, shielding his face from the Redcoat officer. "He's got consumption, Sir!" she said.

The officer let out an oath, shoved his sword back in its scabbard, and pulled a handkerchief from his pocket.

"God help him!" he said in an anguished voice, muffled by the handkerchief he clasped over his mouth and nose.

Then he turned on his heel and pounded down the stairs and out the front door.

Instinctively, Eliza ran after him.

Outside, the Redcoat realized that she was still close at his heels. He wheeled around.

"You *are* like an infernal puppy dog!" he bawled.

The two foot soldiers stood in front of him, smirking. Bessie was tied to the lieutenant's horse and the geese had been let out of the barnyard. They milled around Bessie, squawking and honking excitedly. Bessie let out a loud, plaintive *moooooo*. This agitated the geese even more. Feathers were ruffled. A gander honked loudly and charged at the cow.

The officer's wrath gathered momentum. "I told you to leave the animals alone, man!" he bellowed. "As God is my witness, I'll have you flogged for this!" He roared like an angry bull. There was not a trace of the weariness and reserve Eliza had seen in his face a few minutes earlier. "You know General Tryon's orders—'No looting from those who stand with the King.'"

Then he looked at the clock on top of the woodpile as though he were seeing it for the first time. In a flash, he

drew his sword and with one grand sweep he struck the clock with the flat side of his weapon. The clock sailed a short distance through the air and hit the ground with a crash.

"That clock is more trouble than a three-month baby!" he roared.

The men were silent and sullen. Scraggs' dark eyes

darted sulkily toward his clock, now strewn over the ground in a hundred pieces. He scuffed the dirt angrily, but said nothing.

Jones scowled and muttered, "Others are takin' what suits their fancy."

The lieutenant heard him. The air whistled as his sword swung down again; this time its razor edge cut the rope holding Bessie. The rope snapped like a taut thread.

The officer swung up into his saddle—his back straight,

elbows close to his sides in the manner of an expert horseman.

In a slow, controlled voice he addressed his men. "Now, do you want to reach Compo Beach alive and in time to board ship? Or," he demanded, "do you want to stay in this wretched village?"

With that he flicked the reins and his horse headed back down the lane at a fast trot.

Jones and Scraggs stared after him, smoldering fury in their eyes.

"Come on." Jones spat out the words.

But Scraggs glowered at Eliza. His face was dark with hate. He had been defeated. She had the cow. His precious clock lay broken on the ground, springs and wheels strewn around the woodpile.

He spit on the ground. "Keep that cow where I can get her real easy," he snarled. "I'll be back this evenin'!"

Eliza quailed.

The evil-eyed soldier turned and started down West Lane at a jog. At the far end of the road, Eliza saw the officer waiting, his horse held in check, while the soldiers caught up to him on foot.

Eliza took a deep breath, turned on her heels, and ran back into the house.

Upstairs she sailed into her mother's arms and hugged her with all her might; then she released her and began to turn in circles around the room. As she twirled, she caught sight of Luke, lying in Father's bed, pale as death, and stopped.

Then she pointed her finger at Jeremiah in disbelief. "You!" she cried softly. "Where were *you?* You appear and disappear like a ghost! Where *were* you, Jeremiah?" she persisted.

"Behind the door," Jeremiah answered smugly.

"Behind the door!" Eliza echoed his words. "I don't believe it!"

"Well, I was, silly." Jeremiah pretended to be offended. He reached out and flung back the door so that Eliza could see the bean-pole stretcher leaning against the wall next to the musket.

"Right there," he said, pointing to the stretcher and the gun.

"If that Redcoat lieutenant had discovered the truth we were going to keep him right here with us. Your mother," he grinned at Mrs. Bouton, "was going to disarm him after I took him by surprise with this gun. Then we were going to have him call out the window and order his soldiers to go on ahead alone."

"I don't believe he would have burned our house," Eliza said soberly, "even if he had found out we are rebels. I don't believe he wanted to harm us."

"How can you be sentimental about a Redcoat?" Jeremiah reproved. "He's the King's soldier, and he would have burned this house down to the ground and taken Luke with him," Jeremiah went on indignantly.

"We heard the two foot soldiers talking before you came upstairs. If you hadn't signaled like we were Loyalists I wouldn't be surprised if this house wasn't a sea of flames right now," he concluded vehemently.

Chapter 11

Well!" said Mrs. Bouton in the same tone of voice she used when she had finally knitted the last stitch in a wool sock or shaped a great bowl of bread dough into a dozen loaves and set them out to rise.

Now she looked down at Luke sleeping peacefully in the big bed. "I do believe the boy is looking better," she said with satisfaction. "Perhaps rest and nourishment will restore him after all. I'll go and warm the tea for you children and heat some broth for Luke."

She faced Jeremiah and took his hand affectionately. "I don't know what we would have done without you, son," she said.

Jeremiah grinned sheepishly.

"He's like a member of our family," Eliza blurted and then blushed.

"Well!" repeated Mrs. Bouton, as though she had just finished yet another sock. "Jeremiah, will you go out and see what mischief those two lobsterbacks caused in our barn? At least they didn't notice the root cellar. Eliza, you stay with Luke while I put the kettle on."

Jeremiah spoke to Eliza. "I'll come right back up here and watch Luke soon as I've checked the barn so's you can have tea first."

Eliza nodded, gratefully accepting Jeremiah's gallantry.

Left alone in the room with Luke, she tiptoed to the window. Her petticoat lay beneath it in a heap where it had fallen. She held it up and smiled to herself as she kneeled down to look out the window again. Still holding the petticoat in one hand, she crossed her arms on the windowsill and gazed down on one stray goose waddling near the woodpile amongst the clock parts.

The setting sun cast a red light through the branches of the giant oak tree that grew in front of the house. One low limb reached out like a great arm, almost touching the window with its gnarled fingers. Eliza had often knelt in this place before and watched the birds fly from branch to branch in the old tree. Sometimes a squirrel would scamper up the big trunk and out on the limb, causing the leaves to rustle and tremble. She could watch the squirrels and the birds, only a few feet away, while she remained hidden in the shadows of the room, unnoticed by the little creatures. Sometimes a squirrel would jump from the limb onto the roof of the house and she could hear its tiny feet pattering overhead.

Now the tiny green leaves danced and fluttered lightly in a breeze that slowly lifted the limb up and down. The movement reminded Eliza of an old man nodding his head in church.

Her thoughts went back to Grandmother Hoyt. "That tree was here when Grandmother Hoyt lived in this house," she mused, and an idea began to take shape in her mind. Why, she thought, in a way, Grandmother was alive today. She was helping me wave this red petticoat at the soldiers. And Eliza decided that when a person died his important qualities lived on in others. The real things that are *you* never die, she thought, because you have given them to others—your courage, or diligence, or kindness, or even hate! A cold chill went up her spine and she shivered.

Suddenly she felt very tired. She yearned to close her eyes and sleep. She rested her head on her arms, and warmth and peace hovered over her. Slowly her eyelids closed and she fell asleep. In her dream she stepped down into a hole in the ground. She tried to catch herself to keep from falling and awoke with a jerk. Wearily, she forced herself to raise her head. She couldn't sleep now!

She looked up. Jeremiah was standing next to her. "Your mother has your tea ready," he said.

She nodded, as though still in a dream, and walked downstairs in a daze, leaving Jeremiah with Luke.

It was almost dark. Eliza could never remember such tiredness. She stumbled like a sleepwalker through the kitchen into the spring room, took the long dipper and reached down into the cool depths of the barrel. She drank the cold water from the dipper, then she poured what was left over her fingertips and touched her eyes.

She sat down at the table with her mother and drank the warm cup of tea set before her and tasted the fresh bread, spread with butter and West Indies sugar. Slowly, she felt strength flowing back into her body.

She began to talk, telling her mother about the soldiers and the officer, remembering for herself, aloud, how she had followed at the lieutenant's heels when he went upstairs, then sent him to the wrong room.

Her imagination was kindled by the telling. She described the officer in his wrath. "Mother, he took the broadside of his sword and knocked the clock on the ground! Like this!" Her arm swept an arc through the air.

"When he saw Bessie tied to his saddle, he raged at Jones, and then. . . ." She jumped from her chair and swung the imaginary sword through the air again. "Snap!" she cried. "Bessie was cut free!"

Eliza flopped back onto her chair. She was feeling much better. She leaned across the table, suddenly serious. "Mother, if more soldiers should come, I know we can fool them. And if Jones and Scraggs do come back for Bessie we can frighten them away. They are cowards."

"Perhaps," Mrs. Bouton answered, "your father and Richard will come home soon."

Eliza and Mrs. Bouton fell silent, each preoccupied with her own thoughts. Firelight danced off the pewter mugs on the table. Outside it was pitch black.

Then Mrs. Bouton broke the silence. "We will have to take turns sleeping," she said. "I think we should light a candle in the front bedroom. I'll nurse Luke and look down the lane from the window from time to time. He mumbled something about the message again as Jeremiah and I were carrying him upstairs."

"I wish I were a boy," Eliza said wistfully. "I'd take Luke's message for him."

Then her imagination conjured up a dream. She saw herself galloping down the post road on Melody, her skirts flying out in the wind, and in her vision she was wearing a bright red petticoat. Then she was rapping sharply on an inn door in some faraway town, calling out, "I have a message for General Washington, Sir!" A soldier opened the door and she gave him a brisk salute. . . . "But you're only a girl!" he was saying. . . .

Jeremiah's voice cut the silence and the dream ended. "Mrs. Bouton, Eliza," he called down the stairwell, "Luke is awake!"

81

Eliza took a candle from the table to light the way up-stairs. Luke's eyes were opened wide. The ashes had left dark streaks on the white pillow slip beneath his head. The gloomy shadows of the tall bedposts swayed and danced in the flickering candlelight on the wall behind the bed.

Mrs. Bouton followed Eliza into the room, carrying a steaming bowl of beef broth. Eliza took the pillow next to Luke and gently slipped it under his head so that he could sip the warm soup. Mrs. Bouton fed him. He took the first spoonful eagerly, then another and another, until the bowl was empty.

"Thank you, Ma'am, that was good." Luke smiled gratefully.

"We thank God that you are better, Luke. We've been worried about you." Mrs. Bouton set the bowl down on the candlestand next to the bed. A cool breeze blew in through the window and she pulled the coverlid up to Luke's chin.

"How long has it been?" Luke asked, searching the shadowy faces around him. He had come to the house in the dark and now darkness had fallen again.

"Since early morning," Eliza answered.

Luke frowned. "I must get my message to Dobbs Ferry!" he murmured desperately.

"You've a serious wound. You can't move, Luke." Mrs. Bouton was firm.

Luke stared at the ceiling. "General Wooster trusted me. If only there was someone *I* could trust to take my message the rest of the way."

"I could take it!" Jeremiah's voice was hoarser than ever with excitement.

Mrs. Bouton frowned thoughtfully.

82

"But . . . but I'd hate to leave you two alone!" Jeremiah looked from Mrs. Bouton to Eliza.

Mrs. Bouton laid her hand on Luke's shoulder. "As soon as the sky lightens Jeremiah will go for help or take your message himself. But tonight," she went on earnestly, "the British are all around us. No one could get out of Ridgefield tonight!"

"No one except a girl, like me!" Eliza spoke up. "I can ride as well as a boy," she pleaded, "and nobody would ever suspect me."

Mrs. Bouton looked at Elza reproachfully, but Luke's eyes sparkled thoughtfully. Or so it seemed to Eliza.

But then, looking at Mrs. Bouton, he said resignedly, "Morning will be soon enough."

The conversation had taken all his strength. He closed his eyes and slept.

"Come children," Mrs. Bouton whispered. "Luke will rest comfortably now."

Downstairs, Jeremiah ate heartily while Mother and Eliza sat at the table with him.

"You sure are a good cook, Mrs. Bouton," he ventured, after four slices of bread, two glasses of milk, and a dish of stewed peaches. As he began his second dish of peaches, Eliza absentmindedly toyed with a spoon. She couldn't forget the expression of hate in Scraggs' eyes that afternoon when he had threatened to return for Bessie.

"What will we do if those two soldiers, Scraggs and Jones, do come back?" she blurted out.

Chapter 12

All three agreed. If Scraggs and Jones came back to make trouble, they would be ready to defend themselves, the house, and Luke—with the musket, if need be.

Jeremiah offered to take the first watch, while Mrs. Bouton and Eliza slept in Eliza's room. They bolted the downstairs doors, fastened the windows, blew out the candles, and went upstairs. One small tallow candle glimmered on the candlestand next to Luke's bed. It was the only light in the house.

Jeremiah sat bolt upright in a chair by the window, where he could listen for the warning sounds of voices or footsteps in the lane. His hands rested on the flintlock musket on his knees. Behind him, Luke was sleeping soundly.

In Eliza's room, Mother and Eliza lay down on the bed, fully dressed.

Eliza nestled her head close to her mother's shoulder. The room was as dark as pitch. "Did you take off your shoes?" she asked sleepily.

"No, not even my shoes," Mother answered grimly.

Somewhere in the forest an owl hooted mournfully. In less time than it takes a leaf to float from treetop to earth,

Eliza was asleep—the dreamless, heavy sleep of utter exhaustion, where time stands still.

Downstairs, the hours ticked away on the grandfather clock. Eliza slept on until the earliest hour of the morning. Then, even before time for the cock to crow, she felt herself being awakened.

There was a hand on her shoulder. For a moment she lay, half dazed, trying to remember where she was. The hand shook her shoulder.

"Eliza, wake up!" It was Jeremiah.

Swinging her legs to the floor, she sat for a moment on the edge of the bed. Her clothes clung to her. She felt sticky and warm, the nape of her neck was damp, her feet felt cramped in her shoes, and her hair was tousled. Mechanically, she got up and followed Jeremiah's shadowy form out the door and into the front bedroom.

The candle next to Luke's bed flickered. A fan of gray smoke drifted toward the ceiling and disappeared in the darkness. Eliza looked at Jeremiah. His eyes were red and swollen. He rubbed the heavy lids and yawned.

"It's about four o'clock," he said sleepily. "I tried to stay awake all night, so you and your mother wouldn't have to get up. But," he yawned, "awww, Eliza, I just can't stay awake. I'm afraid I might drop off to sleep without meaning to."

Eliza felt sorry for Jeremiah. "You shouldn't have done that, Jeremiah! Everybody needs some sleep," she said. "But thanks a lot."

Jeremiah flushed. "I guess I'm just not used to staying up all night. Auntie Agnew is a stickler for getting to bed early."

Eliza forced her eyes open wider and tried to look

awake. "I wanted to get up!" she said, glancing at Luke. "Is everything all right?"

Jeremiah nodded. "Just fine," he said. "I reckon I'll lie down right here. You shake me, or kick me, or something, if anything bothers you." He handed her the heavy gun. "Now, don't use this. Wake me!" he insisted. "But just pull back on this trigger if you feel obliged to shoot fast." He grinned. "That musket is almost as big as you," he observed.

"Papa lets me shoot it now and again," she said. Her father had shot a wolf with it one night as the animal carried away a spring lamb. He had caught raccoons in the cornfield and shot them, and he had killed poisonous snakes in the field with it. But never, thought Eliza, has it been aimed at a person.

Jeremiah took a crazy quilt from the foot of the four-poster and rolled it around his big frame. He looked like a long varicolored cocoon, except for a shock of black hair and two big brown eyes peering out the top. Clutching the cover with both hands from the inside, he lay down awkwardly on the floor.

Chapter 13

By the time Eliza tiptoed to the bed to look at Luke and then settled herself on the chair by the window, the sound of deep, heavy breathing from the giant cocoon told her Jeremiah was already sound asleep.

Away off in the woods young foxes yowled shrilly. *"Yip yip yipeee"* they called over and over again. Eliza rested her chin in her hands, elbows on her knees, and gazed outside. The gun was leaning against the window-sill. She felt happy to be sitting in the quiet coolness of the night, with the family sleeping soundly in the shelter of the house. The house itself seemed to her like a ship in an ocean of darkness.

She had enjoyed quiet moments like this for as long as she could remember. Sometimes, after milking the cows, she would stop in the path just to listen to the early morning sounds around her.

Richard never did, but he wasn't made like Eliza. He liked movement and excitement. He never walked when he could run. He never stopped to gaze at a tree; he climbed it. He never lay on his back in the field to study the sky, wondering if he could ever pierce the blueness to something beyond. When Richard looked into the sky, it was to determine whether or not it would be a clear day for hunting.

She thought of him now, somewhere out in the night, probably asleep on the ground with the other militiamen. Or, if he were lucky, in some neighbor's barn, asleep on a bed of hay.

She heard a scratching on the ground below the window and peered down into the bright beady eyes of a big raccoon. She laughed. Raccoons were mischievous creatures. This sly fellow was prowling, looking for a midnight feast. And it would be our hen eggs if he could get at them, Eliza thought.

There was a faint crunching noise in the lane.

"My imagination," she told herself and waited. Then she stiffened and clutched the gun. There was the distinct sound of footsteps approaching the house. The steps quickened to a jog, then a run. As she peered into the inky darkness she heard footfalls fly around the house.

She rushed to Jeremiah's side, grabbed at the quilt and tugged. Jeremiah didn't budge. She pounded his back with her fist and hissed into his ear, "Jeremiah, somebody is here!"

He moaned in his sleep and ducked his head farther down into the cocoon.

Eliza stopped pounding on Jeremiah and listened. There was a voice at the door. She recognized it.

"Papa!" she screamed. The musket clattered onto the bare floor. She raced down the stairs, threw the bolt on the door, and flew into her father's arms.

"Is everything all right?" he asked.

"Everything's fine, Papa!" she assured him.

Eliza could not see her father's face in the dark, but his voice was choked with emotion.

"We must thank God for our blessings this day," he
said. "No one will ever know how I felt to see our house
still standing here."

He squeezed Eliza's shoulders again. "I didn't fully
realize just how much I loved this place—and my girl!"

"How is Richard?" Eliza asked.

"Richard's fine. He is whole and healthy, but hungry,

as usual." He laughed. "Now, quickly, wake your mother."

He knelt by the fire and blew into the coals. They reddened and sparks flew up the chimney as he laid fresh wood on the smoldering embers. Eliza could see his face more clearly in the firelight. It was streaked with dirt and creased with weariness. His breeches were wrinkled and sooty, his shoes caked with dry mud.

He looked up. "What are you waiting for, child?" he asked. "I've only a short time!"

Mrs. Bouton appeared, sleepy-eyed, at the top of the stairs.

"It's all right, Mother," Eliza called up to her. "Papa's home!"

There was a flurry and Mrs. Bouton was down the stairs and in Father's arms. She drew back to look at him full in the face. "You're well, Ebenezer . . . and Richard?"

"Richard's well too. You may be proud of him, Hannah. He is a fine young man. He's with the men in town. Now, what about food for a hungry soldier?" he asked.

Soon the kitchen was filled with the delicious aroma of bread warming and the early morning sounds Eliza was accustomed to hear on a Monday morning—the soft clatter of pewter utensils, spoons thumping the sides of the big black pots that hung over the fire, and water splashing on the stone floor in the spring room.

Breakfast was always early in the summertime, and Eliza loved this magical moment between darkness and day. She thought of the night as a tall, thin form, higher than the treetops, silently sweeping a black cape across the land, gathering all of its dark mysteries under its cloak and stealthily tiptoeing away with them.

April 28 dawned fair and peace enveloped the Boutons'

kitchen. But had Eliza climbed to her crow's nest perch in the tulip tree she would have seen mist rising on the waters of Long Island Sound, and through the shimmering haze she would have seen the sails of the British fleet, gliding across the water like phantoms in the rosy dawn.

The ships were returning to the Connecticut shore to reclaim the horde of red-coated soldiers they had spilled out on the land three days ago.

A house in Ridgefield, burned to the ground during the night, had been the torch that signaled the boats.

Chapter 14

Ebenezer Bouton pulled back his chair at the head of the table and sat down to breakfast.

"The Bradley house was burned to the ground last night," he said.

"Abigail's home! Burned!" Eliza cried.

"And Mrs. Bradley and the children?" Mrs. Bouton asked.

"Mrs. Bradley took the baby and Abigail back in the woods before the Redcoats came. I'm told that the good woman had the foresight to take some of their household goods with her in the wagon.

"But Elisha Bradley is grieved, Hannah, as any man would be. His life's work, used as a torch to signal the British fleet. Now it is nothing more than a few charred boards and a pile of stones."

"Maybe," Eliza ventured softly, "we can help Abby and the Bradleys."

"We will do what we can to help all our neighbors," Mr. Bouton answered gravely. "At least six houses were burned in our village before nightfall."

He bowed his head, and Eliza, bursting with impatience to speak, gazed into her lap while her father said the blessing.

"Now," he said, "I must eat your good meal, Mrs. Bouton, and get back to my regiment."

"Tell us what you can, Ebenezer. *We* are starved for news," said Mrs. Bouton.

"When Richard and I left you at the tavern on Friday, no one was certain where General Tryon and his Redcoats would land, but the rumor was that General Howe had ordered him to destroy all our supplies in Danbury." He shook his head. "And I am afraid the Tory firebrand succeeded in that!"

"Where were you Saturday night in the storm?" Eliza asked.

"We were with General Silliman Saturday. He was on leave in Fairfield when the fleet was spotted."

"Did you see *General Silliman?*" Eliza asked. She knew this famous man was the commander of the Connecticut Militia.

"Yes, my dear, I saw the general," he answered.

"We got to Redding around noon Saturday. General Wooster's troops joined us there later in the afternoon and some seven hundred of us went on to Bethel. We were on the lobsterbacks' tail," he said, "but they were already in Danbury when we got to Bethel. Saturday night was a nightmare. Our powder was ruined by the rain. Half of our muskets wouldn't fire, and the British had gotten word from their spies that we were close."

He spoke rapidly, pausing from time to time to eat.

"The Redcoats set fire to everything! By midnight Danbury was an inferno! All the supplies for our Continental soldiers were burned—four thousand barrels of beef and pork, a thousand barrels of flour, I don't know how many hogsheads of sugar, wheat, oats and corn, thousands of tents, shoes, and stockings!"

93

"We can be thankful, at least, that winter is behind us," Mother said.

Mr. Bouton nodded. "There were thirty pipes of wine and countless puncheons of New England rum. After the British helped themselves to these supplies half their army was drunk."

"I guess there is more than one way to skin a cat," Mrs. Bouton remarked tartly.

"Or befuddle an enemy?" Mr. Bouton smiled and went on. "We were prepared to make the Redcoats pay severely for their sacking. At Bethel we split our forces. Richard and I were sent with General Wooster—there were about two hundred of us—right into Danbury to clean up any stragglers. The rest of the militia under General Benedict Arnold and General Silliman headed due south to cut off the British here in Ridgefield.

"Some two thousand Redcoats had ravaged Danbury. It was a dreadful sight! The stink of burning meat hung in the air, and the fat ran ankle-deep in the streets."

Eliza's eyes widened.

"Enough of that," her father said, covering Mrs. Bouton's hand with his own huge work-worn palm.

"We followed the British right into Ridgefield, but General Wooster was wounded in a skirmish near Lake Mamanasco. I doubt the brave man will live to see the sun set on this day.

"Many brave Patriots died, Hannah, and many Redcoats will never see England again. The battle next to Master Stebbins' house was the worst!"

"I suppose you must go back?" Mrs. Bouton asked softly.

"We will follow the British right back to the Sound and prod them from the rear every mile of the way," he said grimly. "I suppose General Washington has received the news by now. He was counting on those Danbury supplies."

"Luke!" Eliza suddenly exclaimed, looking at her mother. "I had forgotten him until Papa mentioned General Washington! And Jeremiah is still asleep on the floor!"

"And I doubt that a cannon would wake the boy now," said Mrs. Bouton. "Finish your meal, child, I'll look after Luke."

"Jeremiah? Luke?" Mr. Bouton echoed the names. "Who might they be?" he demanded.

"It's all right, Ebenezer," Mrs. Bouton soothed.

"You know Jeremiah," Eliza chimed in.

95

"Do you mean that gangling nephew of Miss Agnew's, the one who fell in the well last summer?" he asked. "Is *he* here now?"

"Yes, Papa. He has been a great help to us. Together we saved Luke from the Redcoats!"

"Do you mean the British came *here*, child?" Mr. Bouton looked around the room in disbelief. "Pray tell me, Hannah, who is Luke?"

"Luke is a Patriot soldier, just a boy, Ebenezer, and he found refuge here in our home. He is badly wounded, and it was Eliza's quick thinking that saved him, and us, from the British." She smiled. "Eliza and her red petticoat!"

"I waved my petticoat out the window," explained Eliza. "And since it was red the soldiers thought we were Tories! And they thought Luke was *you!* That is why our house wasn't burned."

Ebenezer Bouton's face turned crimson with anger.

"Tories!" he roared. "You let the British think that we are Tories?" He pounded his fist on the table. "Woman, far better to have this house destroyed than to be suspected of being a Tory!"

Tears welled in Eliza's eyes. She had never seen her father lose his temper like this. He was usually a gentle man, and he had not been so bitter about Tories before. She felt angry, hurt, and betrayed.

Mrs. Bouton spoke hotly. "Ebenezer, please speak to the soldier before you berate your family." She motioned up the stairs. "He is resting in your bed."

Without saying another word, Ebenezer Bouton, his head bowed, trudged up the stairs. Eliza heard the bedroom door shut, then the hum of voices from above. When Mr. Bouton came back downstairs, he went directly to Eliza, put his arm around her tiny shoulders, and said, "Please forgive me. You had no choice. Luke had to be saved—and his message too."

He looked at Mrs. Bouton and grinned. "She is resourceful, isn't she, like any Hoyt!" Then, turning back to Eliza, he asked, "Did you know that if the British had captured Luke out of uniform he would have been strung up as a spy?"

"Hanged?" Eliza whispered.

Mr. Bouton nodded and squeezed her shoulder, "Never mind, Eliza, Luke is safe now, thanks to you and your mother and Jeremiah." He paused and smiled. "You were right, my dear, Jeremiah *is* sound asleep—and dreaming. Mumbled something in his sleep while I was upstairs. Sounded as though he said 'Not yet, Daddy!'"

"Jeremiah was dreaming about the battle in Ridgefield yesterday, Papa. He saw General Arnold's horse shot from under him!"

Mr. Bouton frowned thoughtfully. "It seems that the soldiers are not the only ones involved in this war," he said, walking to the window. It was light outside now. The clock said six. Eliza and her mother stood, motionless, waiting for him to speak again.

Eliza knew he was thinking, thinking of how to get Luke's message to Dobbs Ferry. He clasped his hands behind his back. Slowly, he rubbed his thumb back and forth across one palm.

Then, abruptly, he turned around and faced his wife. "Hannah, please, get the ink and a quill and a piece of paper. I have a message to add to Luke's.

"Luke was carrying important information from our Patriots in Boston. I must add what I know about the supplies destroyed at Danbury and General Wooster, God save him! Luke was given the message by Wooster. Now the poor man may be dead."

Mrs. Bouton fumbled nervously in the cupboard drawer. "We've no paper, Ebenezer. I'll have to tear a page from the diary," she said.

She set the ink bottle and turkey quill in front of Mr. Bouton, along with a blank sheet of paper from the diary and a small piece of sealing wax.

His hand moved rhythmically across the paper. Every Sabbath evening since Eliza could remember, her father sat at the table, writing in large, bold script, his weekly account of crops, weather, and livestock. "It's a farm diary," he said once, "so we can profit from experience."

Eliza often pored over the diary. It was fun to find out if the first frost had come so early the previous fall or to read exactly when the geese flew north last year.

Her father's quill scratched over the paper and soon both sides were filled.

"I'll need another blank sheet, please," he said.

He covered the first sheet of paper with the blank piece, then folded and sealed the two with wax.

"Now," he said, leaning back in the chair, "Luke's man at Dobbs Ferry is a ferryboat captain. Hawley is his name—Rufus Hawley."

"Father," Eliza ventured, "I could take the message." She touched the folded paper. "Jeremiah could go with me," she said. "Together we would be safe!"

Mr. Bouton motioned to a chair opposite him. "Sit down, Hannah," he said, spreading his large, brown hands out, palms flat on the table. He studied his hands. "I've been thinking," he said slowly. "Eliza and Jeremiah may have to go!" He looked up into Mrs. Bouton's eyes.

Eliza saw her mother stiffen and watched the color drain from her cheeks.

"Hannah," he soothed, "there is no other way. Please, hear me out, I have a plan!"

Chapter 15

I have a scheme for getting these messages to Dobbs Ferry with Eliza and Jeremiah!" Mr. Bouton's voice was edged with excitement. "Please, Hannah, you must realize that the fate of our Continental army depends on information of this sort!" He pressed the folded paper beneath his hand.

Eliza knew by the look in her mother's eyes and by the way that she tilted her chin upward that she did not like the idea. But Eliza knew too that her mother would gracefully accept what was inevitable.

"Tell me, child," Mr. Bouton went on, "do you remember the road we took last summer when we visited Uncle Joseph in Dobbs Ferry?"

Eliza nodded solemnly. She would never forget the trip—or the road! The family had gone in the wagon. The twenty-five miles had taken all day, but she had loved every minute of it. She and Richard had taken turns sitting up on the buckboard with her father. They had passed big farms, two inns, and several hamlets before they came to Dobbs Ferry, nestled on the shore of the Hudson River. The trip had been the most exciting thing in her whole life—up until yesterday.

They had stayed three days in Dobbs Ferry to help with a barn raising and to visit. Then they had come home. Of course she remembered the road!

"Good," said Mr. Bouton. "The matter is settled. You will ride Melody and Jeremiah can ride Brownie." He smiled. "At least I trust he can ride Brownie."

"We can be there by nightfall!" Eliza said.

"Good girl," her father said.

"Now listen carefully. . . ." He stopped. "Better still, wake up Jeremiah. Quickly, child!"

Soon a sleepy-faced Jeremiah stumbled down the stairs behind Eliza.

He looks like an old owl, Eliza thought as Jeremiah shook hands with her father.

"I hear you've helped the womenfolk in my house, Jeremiah," said Mr. Bouton. "God bless you, boy."

"Thank you, Sir." Jeremiah's voice sounded as though he were stepping on acorns, but Eliza noticed that he looked straight into her father's eyes.

Mr. Bouton motioned to Jeremiah to sit down at the table. "This letter," he said, touching the sealed message he had just written, "contains information about the sacking of Danbury and the movement of General Tryon's troops. Luke's letter is sewn in his jacket. It is more important than you may have realized. I spoke to the boy while you slept upstairs."

Jeremiah nodded. "And Luke's jacket must still be under your bed, Sir!"

Jeremiah looked at Mrs. Bouton and smiled. Eliza knew the three of them would never forget the scene in the upstairs bedroom when the British officer stomped into the room and saw Luke's shoe on the floor.

"Hannah," Mr. Bouton said, "would you get Luke's jacket from under my bed and cut the message from it?"

Mrs. Bouton started up the stairs.

"And, Hannah," her husband called after her, "please

don't worry about cutting the jacket. Time is more important now!"

Eliza knew her father was thinking of her mother's thrift. Even at a time like this, she thought briefly, Mother would not want to ruin a good jacket.

"Jeremiah," Mr. Bouton continued, "would you ride with Eliza to Dobbs Ferry to deliver these messages to a man called Hawley at the ferry?"

Jeremiah brightened. Suddenly, he no longer looked sleepy. "Yes, Sir!" he said loudly.

"Good," said Mr. Bouton. "With luck, you can be there by nightfall. You will take only a handkerchief of food and a bag of oats for the horses. You should have time to rest yourselves at noon."

He turned to Eliza. "If you can't find the ferryman, go to your Uncle Joseph. He'll help you."

Eliza nodded.

"Now," he commanded, "both of you stand by the fire! Hurry! Time is short."

Eliza looked at Jeremiah. Obediently the two went to the fireplace.

"Eliza, take off your apron and catch the ribbon on fire. Jeremiah, rub some soot on your face and hold your jerkin over the fire. You two children had your home burned by the lobsterbacks!"

Jeremiah whisked his doublet through the fire and then dabbed his fingertips in the black soot at the edge of the fireplace. Eliza swiped her hand across the inky black powder and touched it to her cheek. Then the two rebels stared at one another and grinned.

Mrs. Bouton appeared, carrying a wrinkled sheet of paper, folded and sealed. She stopped abruptly and stared at the children.

"Ezenezer, *what* in this world. . . ."

"These two children had their house burned by the British, Hannah, and they are going to Dobbs Ferry to stay with their relations until we can go for them," Mr. Bouton said. "You see, my dear, it's part of my plan!"

"I see," she answered crisply, "that the Hoyts are not the only resourceful members of this family!"

Eliza smiled to herself.

Mr. Bouton poked the fire and a cloud of smoke blew out into the kitchen. "Good," he said, "now you smell like smoke.

"Don't gallop the horses. That would only attract attention to yourselves. If you meet anyone on the road, make your manners, but tell only what you are asked and don't change your story."

He looked at Mrs. Bouton. "Don't worry, Hannah, no one will ever suspect that they are carrying military information," he said.

"But how will they hide these letters, Ebenezer?" she asked. "Perhaps," she implored, "it would not be so dangerous if the messages were hidden. But this way. . . ." Her voice trailed off and Eliza saw her mother's lips tremble.

"I know how to hide them!" Eliza cried, and bounded up the stairs two at a time. When she reappeared a second later she was carrying her red petticoat. "Mother, we could sew the letters into this!" She held the petticoat out to her mother.

Jeremiah shuffled his feet and his face turned the color of the petticoat.

"Now that *that* is settled, Jeremiah, shall the two of us saddle your horses?" Mr. Bouton asked.

Mrs. Bouton took out her sewing box and with basting stitches she neatly tacked the two papers to the petticoat, about six inches above the ruffle, one on either side. Then she took two pieces of the same red cloth and deftly whipped patches over the messages.

Eliza stepped into her petticoat and pulled it up under the smoke-stained calico skirt.

"I'll be right back," she called out, darting upstairs again. She tiptoed to Luke's bedside. His eyes were closed.

"Luke," she said softly, "we're taking your message to Dobbs Ferry now. I wanted to tell you."

Luke opened his eyes and smiled. "Hawley at the ferryboat landing?"

Eliza nodded. "Don't worry, Luke, we'll get it there safely."

"Your pa told me he would see it was delivered," he said and closed his eyes.

Outside, Jeremiah was mounted on Brownie. Eliza threw her skirts over one arm, put her foot in the stirrup, and swung up onto Melody's back.

Mrs. Bouton was tying a kerchief of food to the saddle.

Eliza's eyes sparkled with excitement. Jeremiah, looking like a scarecrow in the saddle, grinned and stroked Brownie's mane.

Mr. Bouton reached up and put his hand on the boy's arm. "Good luck, and Godspeed, boy," he said. "Take care of my girl!"

Eliza leaned down and kissed her mother's cheek. Mrs. Bouton stood silently, her lips trembling.

Mr. Bouton grasped Melody's reins close over the mare's neck to stay the horse a moment longer. He looked up at Eliza. "Godspeed, take care, child," he cried. Then abruptly, he let go of the reins and gave the horse a loud slap across the rump.

Melody broke into a trot, followed by Jeremiah on

Brownie, down West Lane. Neither Eliza nor Jeremiah glanced back until they came to the spot where the British officer had paused to wait for his men.

Here they halted their horses. They could see Mother and Father standing arm in arm, each with a hand lifted in farewell. Eliza and Jeremiah waved back.

Then Eliza leaned forward in her saddle, Jeremiah prodded Brownie with his heel, and they headed for the winding road to Dobbs Ferry at a fast trot.

Chapter 16

The late afternoon sun cast a rosy light on everything it touched and cut a wide swath of pink and silver across the glimmering waters of the stately Hudson River.

Eliza contemplated the undulating hills on the opposite shore. Bare brown trees fringed their top edges, looking to her like delicate bristles brushing the sky. The hillsides were as stark and brown as they must have been in the cold, dreary months of February and March. Only the warmth of the sun on her head hinted that April had come to the colony of New York.

Eliza's shoulders sagged. Her shoe had rubbed a raw, burning blister on her ankle and her fingers ached from holding Melody's reins all day. She wished desperately that they could stop and rest, but Jeremiah determinedly prodded Brownie on.

North of Tarrytown, a weathered board sign, with an arrow pointing southward on the Albany Post Road, had told them that "Dobbs—His Ferry" was ahead. They had skirted Tarrytown, finding their way along a narrow footpath on a bluff above the town so as to avoid an encounter with anyone.

The town lay close to the river—a few buildings nestled

among the trees. From their vantage point Eliza and Jeremiah had not seen anyone moving.

"Not even a cow or a horse!" Eliza had commented as she surveyed the bare patch of land framing one brown rooftop. She felt as though they had come upon a settlement from which all had fled, taking with them livestock and wagons.

Now Tarrytown lay behind them. The tired horses, heads drooping, clumped single file along one narrow rut of the wagon road that led along the east bank of the river to Dobbs Ferry.

Eliza stroked Melody's sweating neck, then studied the brown horsehairs that stuck to her own damp palm. She wiped her hand across her skirt, then blew on her cramped fingers.

"You poor horse," she murmured sympathetically. Then, frowning at Jeremiah's back, she muttered, "I may be impatient, but *he* is just plain stubborn."

Then, for the tenth time that day, she reached down and moved her fingers through the folds of her skirt, searching for the stiff rectangles of paper that lay beneath. She knew the messages for General Washington were securely stitched in her petticoat, but still she sighed with relief when her hand touched the cloth patches and the paper. She had felt her responsiblity more and more with each mile that separated them from Luke and from Ridgefield.

These messages weigh on me as though I were dragging two stones the size of bread loaves, she thought wearily.

Her shoe again scraped across the tender skin on her ankle. Wincing, she was about to call out to Jeremiah to stop when his horse halted in the path ahead. He swung around in the saddle and waved excitedly.

Eliza lifted the reins and clicked softly to Melody. With a sudden spurt of energy, the horse trotted forward and stopped abreast of Brownie.

"Look yonder!" Jeremiah drawled, pointing southward.

Trembling with excitement, Eliza quickly scanned the shoreline, looking anxiously toward New York City, but she saw only brown trees trimming the edge of the wide river.

"I can't see a thing!" she cried. "Besides, I'm not nearly high enough!" She stiffened her back to make herself as tall as possible and eagerly surveyed the shoreline once again.

"Sometimes, Eliza, people look too far ahead," Jeremiah said.

Eliza's eyes darted back up the river.

"Now I see it!" she cried. "It *must* be the ferry! And it's as big as Noah's ark!"

Downstream a short distance, a pier extended into the water. Next to it floated a great, flat wooden rectangle, longer and wider than any house Eliza had ever seen.

Eliza and Jeremiah gazed at the boat in awe. A wagon stood on one side of the expansive deck and two bare masts towered overhead. The giant vessel floated on the water so quietly that Eliza thought of it as a wounded whale. The only sign of life in the tableau below them was a thin column of smoke curling up from a narrow strip of sand that separated the river from the dark mass of brush and trees along the shore.

"There *must* be someone there," Eliza said, breaking the silence.

Jeremiah nodded.

Both horses headed down the rocky trail, then stopped

again at a fork in the road. The wagon trail they were traveling slanted down the slope at an angle toward the water, but a footpath branched off sharply to their right, heading straight over the embankment and down to the beach, where now they saw a small fire.

They watched, silently, as a bulky, brown-clad form emerged from the brush and squatted next to the fire with his back to the embankment.

Jeremiah swung quietly down from his saddle and motioned to Eliza to dismount. Holding Brownie's reins in one hand, he held out his other hand to help her.

"You hold the horses," he said softly, handing her both sets of reins. "I'll go down first and find out if that is Hawley."

Eliza nodded and Jeremiah started down the steep incline.

"Jeremiah!" Eliza whispered after him.

He turned around, frowning, and came back to where she stood holding the two horses.

"Suppose this isn't Hawley, suppose it's a Tory—or, a cowboy!" she blurted out.

"Who told *you* about cowboys?" asked Jeremiah.

"I heard Papa telling Richard about them one day," she answered.

She had been in the hayloft when Richard and her father entered the barn, and she had listened as the two talked about the desperadoes who roamed the "neutral ground" in Westchester County. "Cowboys" and "skinners" was what Mr. Bouton had called the marauders, who, he told Richard, rode about the countryside in pairs or little bands, stealing, killing, and burning houses. The words "cruel outlaws" and "bandits without mercy" had drifted up to her nest in the hay.

Now she remembered these words and trembled at the sight of the form huddled over the fire.

Jeremiah hesitated and looked at Eliza sympathetically. "Don't worry. I'll be right back," he assured her, and without waiting for a reply he started down the steep path and disappeared in the trees and brush. Eliza listened to the clumping and scratching noises of his boots fade away down the trail.

Nervously, she squeezed both horses' reins in her fist and strained to get a better look at the figure kneeling before the little fire.

"Please, let this man be Hawley," she prayed silently, as she waited for Jeremiah to emerge on the beach.

While she watched, the man straightened up and looked out at the river before him. Eliza wondered if he had heard Jeremiah.

Then, abruptly, the figure wheeled around. Eliza gasped. A knife blade flashed in the sun. The stranger was moving in a crouched position, slowly, toward the path. He held the knife waist high in front of his body.

Terror-stricken, she saw him stop, dead still, poised like a lion stalking its prey.

Her mouth opened to cry out a warning, but no sound came from her throat. She fought to get her voice. Then, a shrill scream ripped the silence and she heard herself, as though from far over the mountain, calling to Jeremiah.

The scream set her feet in motion. She bounded down the path, following the steep route Jeremiah had taken a few seconds earlier. A thorn bush clawed her skirt and she was caught short. Frantically, she tugged at her snagged dress and yanked it free.

She leaped forward again, blindly—and tripped. She felt herself pitched to the ground and she was tumbling head over heels, down the embankment, plunging straight toward the figure holding the knife.

As she rolled to a stop, a sharp pain wrenched her shoulder and she lay helplessly entangled in a mass of red petticoat and calico. Then a rough hand grasped hers and she was jerked up on her feet to face the strangest looking man she had ever seen.

Spellbound, she stared at the man's shining, moon-shaped face. Dumbfounded, the man looked directly into Eliza's blue eyes.

The stranger was hardly taller than she. His glowing countenance wavered before her eyes. She blinked. It was as though she were looking at the rippling reflection of a face in a flowing brook. Slowly, the man's form came into focus. She saw a shaggy head of reddish-brown hair and tiny beads of sweat glistening on his forehead. A frown drew his heavy brows together and his tiny eyes sparkled fiercely.

Eliza quivered with fear. The man clutched the knife menacingly. Then, slowly, his arm relaxed, his hand dropped to his side, and his stocky form began to vibrate. A low rumbling came from somewhere in his chest. Gradually, his features contorted into a smile. Then he threw back his head and roared with laughter.

His eyes were tiny slits, tilted up at the corners, and his grin was grotesque. One front tooth was broken off and he stuck the tip of his red tongue into the gaping space. His round cheeks were smooth and apple red, but a stubble of beard covered his chin and jaw.

He placed his chubby fists on his stomach and guffawed. Gleefully, he stamped a foot on the hard sand; then he sat down, gasping for breath.

"A girl!" he cried hoarsely. He looked at Eliza's di-

sheveled skirt, torn at the hem to reveal a triangle of red underskirt.

"A girl with a red petticoat!" he chortled.

At the same moment, Eliza caught sight of Jeremiah emerging from the brush behind the stranger. He held a large plank with both hands, ready to strike the rotund stranger over the head.

"A whippersnapper of a girl!" the man repeated, shaking his head.

Still unaware of Jeremiah's menacing form behind him,

he squinted one eye and studied her face seriously. She tried to smile, but her lips trembled and her heart pounded with a deafening thud. Desperately, she tried to keep from looking over his head, to Jeremiah's grim countenance.

Suddenly, the stranger plunged his knife blade into the sand and grinned again.

"My name is Hawley, Missy, Rufus Hawley. I'm pleased to get to know ye," he said.

Jeremiah's plank dropped to the ground with a thud. Hawley let out an oath and swung around, on his feet in an instant.

Eliza covered her ears.

"We have a message for you, Sir—Hawley!" Jeremiah hollered.

"Do ye now?" Hawley said sarcastically, glowering at Jeremiah.

"Please, Sir," Jeremiah implored. "We had to be sure it was *you!*"

Hawley stepped back and riveted his eyes on the boy. Jeremiah shuffled his feet self-consciously. Eliza's fingers danced across her skirt, trying to feel the messages in her underskirt. For a moment no one spoke. Eliza heard the fire snap. A seagull called from high overhead.

Then Hawley broke the silence.

"Guests," he said slowly, with mock gravity, "milady and gentleman. If ye'll allow me now, the dinner here needs tendin' to. Please make yerselves to feel at home here in me kitchen." He motioned pompously to the beach and fire.

A spit had been rigged above the fire and three small birds, quail, Eliza thought, were sizzling and smoking on it.

"Would ye care to join me?" asked Hawley. "It's like I was expectin' ye—almost." He motioned with mock courtliness to the three roasting fowl.

Eliza clutched her skirt and watched, impatiently, as Hawley ambled to the river's edge and took a handful of oysters from a tow sack. Carefully, he laid the oysters in a bed of seaweed on the fire and sat down, cross-legged, on the sand. Once settled comfortably, he drew a flask from somewhere in his ill-fitting homespun shirt and took a draught.

"Ahhhh," he sighed with satisfaction as he wiped his mouth across the back of his sleeve. He slewed his eyes at Jeremiah and held out the flask. Jeremiah declined, grinning sheepishly.

"I'm just plain hungry," he said, eyeing the fire.

The sharp pain stabbed Eliza's shoulder again and she grit her teeth. She wanted to cry, but she lifted her skirt instead, high enough to uncover the stiff patches on her petticoat.

Hawley stopped poking the fire and gaped as she leaned over and picked at the fine, tight stitches Mrs. Bouton had whipped around the edges of each piece of cloth that morning. But her anxious fingers could not find a loose thread. She wanted to rip the papers from her petticoat, but she could not pull a single thread.

Impetuously, she ran toward the riverbank, out of the firelight and into the shadows, where she unbuttoned her underskirt and let it drop down around her ankles. She stepped out of the crimson circle and gathered the cloth up in her arms. For a moment she clutched it to her heart. Then, ruefully, she shook it out and folded it into a small bundle.

"Here are our messages, sir—for General Washington.

My mother sewed them to my petticoat," she said softly as she thrust the red bundle at the ferryman.

Hawley did not laugh, as Eliza half expected he would. Instead, he took the crumpled cloth and stuffed it into the skin pouch he wore over one shoulder.

"Ye'r messages'll be safe right here in me ditty bag," he said, slapping the pouch, "and they'll be even safer in your—ahemm—red petticoat!"

Jeremiah pulled off his jerkin and spread it out on the sand near the fire. "Come on, Eliza, you can rest and be thankful that the messages are delivered at last!" He motioned for her to sit down. "I'll get the horses."

"And ye can tell me ye'r story when ye've eaten," Hawley added.

Jeremiah headed up the embankment. Hawley and Eliza were left alone on the beach. The air was cool. The sun, a great saucer of orange fire, slipped behind the steep cliffs of traprock across the river.

Eliza sighed softly and gazed into the fire. Hawley forked the roasting quail from the skewer and laid the birds on a smooth stone. Their savory smell was wafted into the air and Eliza's mouth watered when he held out a piece of the delicate meat for her to taste. Gingerly, he lifted the oysters from the seaweed and one by one put them on the stone next to the quail. Expertly, he began to eat the oysters from the half shells.

Eliza was too exhausted to speak. The fire snapped. The river gently slapped the beach and a phoebe called sadly from its perch on a hemlock tree.

Eliza listened for the little bird's mate to answer from somewhere in the darkening woods, but instead there was a crashing noise on the embankment. Hawley dropped his oyster shell, grabbed the knife, and wheeled around to face the bank.

Jeremiah emerged from the brush, leading Brownie and Melody. The horses clumped behind him to the river's edge where he held the reins while they drank.

"Well, I'm a three-toed mackerel!" Hawley said dryly. "This ain't no ordinary evenin' for a ferryman!" He sat down, drew the flask from his shirt and upended it. A drop of the brown liquid trickled down one glistening red cheek and stopped at the stubble of beard.

He wiped his mouth and eyed the horses curiously as Jeremiah tied them to a tree. "How far have ye two come?" he asked.

"We've ridden some thirty miles today," Jeremiah answered.

Hawley's eyes narrowed. "Through no-man's-land?"

"Some of it was neutral ground, Sir, Jeremiah said. "We came from the north and east of here—Ridgefield, in the colony of Connecticut. Those messages for General Washington are from General Wooster and Mr. Bouton."

Jeremiah nodded at Eliza. "Mr. Bouton's her pa," he explained. "Luke was carrying General Wooster's message when—"

"Luke! Where's Luke now?" the ferryman demanded.

"He's lying in her pa's bed right now." Jeremiah's voice cracked and he cleared his throat.

Hawley raised his bushy brows and regarded Jeremiah. "I know Luke, son, I carried his messages before! Is he sick?"

"Wounded, Sir, after the British sacked Danbury!" Jeremiah answered.

Then he told the ferryman about Luke and how he and

Eliza had come to be the ones to deliver the important messages.

When he had finished, Hawley contemplated the river thoughtfully. Then he flashed a snaggletoothed grin at Eliza.

"Ye're a brave lady," he said. "That majestic river coursin' behind ye, little one, is a queen." He laughed softly to himself. "I vow ye're as noble as me river, Princess!"

Eliza flushed at Hawley's gallantry. The river was grand, she thought.

On the opposite shore, the palisades jutted straight up out of the water, gigantic slabs of pink rock ripped apart by a glacier thousands of years ago. The gentle foot-hills of the Catskill Mountains met the jagged stone wall at a spot directly across from the ferry landing. The wall extended southward and the hills reached northward as far as she could see. Eliza knew that farther north the fort at West Point commanded the river. Directly south lay Manhattan Island, and at its tip the city of New York, now overrun with Tories playing host to British officers. And along the Hudson's shore to the north of Dobbs Ferry stretched the magnificent domains of the two great landowning families in Westchester—the Philipses and Van Cortlandts.

"Some rivers is queenly, like some ladies," Hawley mused. "A lady owns this ferry," he continued. "Mollie Sneeden's her name."

He paused, then pointed to the ferry. "Never see'd a pettiauger like that one, I'll wager," he said. "Well, Mollie can sail that boat across the flats in a strong tide good as any man." He paused while Jeremiah put a piece of wood into the embers. Bright sparks shot up and disappeared in the night.

"Mollie's a little one too, like ye, Princess," he went on gently. "But she has the courage of some men twice her size."

Eliza gazed at the boat's shadowy form and wondered about Mollie Sneeden. Hawley talked on.

Why, he's plain glad to have someone to keep him company, Eliza thought.

"Did ye know," the ferryman continued, "the Patriots stretched a mighty chain right across this river, shore to shore? Tried to stop the British fleet, they did. Then they loaded hulks with stones and sunk 'em right out there!" He pointed to the river. "But the warships keep comin'. Still them Tories with their fancy navy ain't captured this queen river."

"Did you ever see General Washington?" Jeremiah interjected.

"That I didn't," Hawley said. "But Lady Martha Washington rode her chariot on m'ferry once on a visit to the general!"

Eliza's eyes widened, and Hawley embellished his story. "Caused a flutter, it did," he said proudly "There was Lady Washington, sittin' in her fancy carriage behind four prancin' white horses, with a coachman and a postillion duded out in scarlet and white. I took 'em across, steady, like they was sleddin' over ice." Hawley beamed.

Eliza stared into the fire, imagining the great event.

"But what about Dobbs?" Jeremiah asked.

"Dobbs came from Long Island. Started this ferry 'fore the turn of the century—1698 I reckon it was. But the Dobbses sold out to the Sneedens."

Hawley stopped talking and peered across the fire into Eliza's wan face. Freckles stood out like brown pinpricks on her nose. The streak of soot from the Bouton fireplace was smeared across one pale cheek. Dark circles rimmed her eyes.

"I've rambled on." Hawley sounded embarrassed. "Ferryin' and fishin' can be a lonesome life. Makes talkers out of river folk," he said.

He slapped his thigh. "Now I'll be off with ye'r messages in me private ship," he said, pointing to a skiff rocking gently at the dock.

"Her sail's as dark as a stormy night. She glides across the water like a patch of fog and makes less of a ripple than a water bug." He winked. "I'll have ye'r information in the right hands on the other side before the hoot owl comes out of his nest up there." He motioned toward the dark woods. "By mornin' General Washington'll be in ye'r debt," he said.

Then the ferry captain showed Jeremiah and Eliza a small cave in the embankment. They agreed that Jeremiah would keep the fire going and tend the horses while Eliza slept in the cave.

"Crawl into me own private sleepin' quarters," Hawley said, wrapping a great shaggy bearskin around her shoulders. "If the tide is gentle, I'll send ye both on ye'r way before sunup."

"But what about Aunt—" Eliza started to protest.

Hawley shook his head.

"I'll not be responsible for ye, Princess, if ye go lookin' for aunts and uncles. Ye'll head straight back to Ridgefield at the crack of dawn. Ye'r auntie'll be better off, if ye do." He looked significantly at the horses. Eliza knew he was thinking of the cowboys.

Suddenly, she felt a great affection for the gentle, rough ferryman. "Thank you, Sir—Hawley," she said softly.

"And don't ye be frightened by me animal friends," he added gruffly. "I know a few raccoons—come down every night to share me oysters—not to mention a woodchuck or two and a weasel family."

Then the ferryman pulled a fur cap down over his

shaggy head, shifted the pouch on his shoulder, and headed for the dock, followed by Jeremiah.

The moon had risen and the rippling water of the Hudson sparkled in its light. A breeze blew shoreward, causing tiny waves to splash across the beach.

Eliza sat in the mouth of the black cave and watched Hawley and Jeremiah, silhouetted against the wide expanse of water. Jeremiah gave the boat a shove and Hawley hoisted the sail.

The last thing Eliza remembered was watching the tiny sail glide swiftly over the dark water and disappear into the night. Stars twinkled overhead, and she slept soundly, curled up in the soft bearskin.

Chapter 17

I f only, Eliza thought, I could climb a little higher I might be able to see the Hudson from here! She grabbed hold of an upper branch of the tulip tree. The rough bark felt warm under her hand and the sun was so bright that the budding leaves sparkled like silver.

This was the first time she had climbed to her lookout since she had watched the British warships sail toward the Connecticut coast. Now, as she pulled herself up higher and higher in the tree, her thoughts were with Hawley back at Dobbs Ferry and the beautiful Hudson River.

For without even trying, ever since she and Jeremiah had returned to Ridgefield Eliza kept recalling the ferryman. She saw him, in her mind's eye, sailing across the moonlit river in his little skiff, with the precious messages and her red petticoat stuffed in his "ditty bag."

"Two days at home," she mused, "and it seems like a dream!"

Her thoughts kept going back to Hawley for she wanted to meet him again someday. He had come back across the river that night to assure her and Jeremiah that he had delivered the messages to the "right person" on the other side. "General Washington will have ye'r information by noon this day!" he had said heartily. Then

he had stirred up the embers in his fire and cooked a breakfast of fried fish and corn cakes. After they had eaten he
had gone with them as far as Tarrytown.

He had ridden Melody and Eliza had ridden behind
Jeremiah on Brownie. Hawley's feet barely touched the
stirrups. "I'm more t'home on a boat, where me feet rests
on the planks!" he said seriously. The sun was just peeping
over the horizon, barely lighting the trail when Hawley
rolled off Melody's back and planted his feet on the rocky
path. "Ye're soon out of cowboy territory," he said to
Jeremiah. "Take care of ye'r brave lady here!" Then he
wheeled around and the last time Eliza saw him he was
trudging back down the road to the river's shore, his
boat, and his animal friends.

Now Eliza pulled herself up to a precarious perch in
the tulip tree and searched the skyline in the west. The
Hudson River still was hidden from view by the rolling
hills that separated it from Ridgefield. A huge black bird
appeared in the sky, flapped its powerful wings and glided
over the treetops. "Only a crow can see the river from
here," Eliza muttered.

The tree swayed with a sudden gust of wind and she
knew it was impossible to climb any higher. She hugged
the tree trunk with her arm and turned to face the east.
She cupped one hand over her eyes and gazed intently
at the Sound. Its surface sparkled in the noon sun and
one small sail skimmed its surface.

Satisfied with what she had seen, Eliza leaned forward
and looked down at the ground beneath her. Jeremiah sat
cross-legged in a patch of grass in the shade of the tree.
Even his gangling frame looked small from the treetop,
but she could see his head tilted down in such a way that
she knew he was engrossed in the little volume of *Canter-*

bury Tales. The dragoon he was whittling probably was back in his breeches pocket, nesting next to his knife. His spindly silhouette, all elbows and knees, reminded Eliza of a grasshopper.

She grinned mischievously, reached into her apron pocket and drew out a shiny red apple. She held the fruit by its stem and stared down at the "grasshopper" below, calculating just how far out she would have to cast the apple in order to have it land near her target.

She saw that it probably would careen off a branch in its descent, but she let go anyway. It bounced off two branches and landed on the hillside just above Jeremiah. She watched the red speck tumble down the incline and stop just short of the boy.

She laughed. "If he knew it was something to eat he would notice," she said to herself.

The deep-toned sound of a conch-shell horn reverberated in the town. Eliza watched Jeremiah sit up straight, then stretch his arms skyward. He reached out and picked up the apple, then squinted up into the tree. "Since when did apples fall from tulip trees?" he called.

"It's manna from heaven," Eliza called back, and started her scrambling descent.

"Did you see anything interesting?" Jeremiah said as she swung to the ground from the bottom limb of the tree.

"Only one sail and endless blue water!" she answered breathlessly. "I couldn't see the Hudson."

The two headed back toward West Lane, Eliza skipping and dancing to keep up with Jeremiah's strides. He slowed his pace and smiled. "I guess I'm in too much of a hurry for dinner," he said. "I sure hope your ma has peach pie!"

Jeremiah had been working in the fields with Richard and Father all morning. It had been decided that he would stay with the Boutons for a time. He had eagerly offered to help with the spring planting and Mr. Bouton had seemed more than pleased at the offer.

As they walked silently down the lane, Eliza thought about Jeremiah's new nephew in South Salem. They had stopped there on the trip back from Dobbs Ferry, so that Jeremiah could see his aunt and sister. Eliza had peered, fascinated, into the pine cradle that held the red-faced, puckered baby boy, and she had not been able to resist touching his tiny star-shaped hands.

Her thoughts darted to the noonday meal awaiting them. She loved company. Now there were seven at the table, counting Luke, who still was too weak to travel, and Abigail, who had come to stay with them because now the Bradleys had no home. Mrs. Bradley had taken Abigail's baby brother with her to the Meads until a new house could be built, perhaps on the very spot where the old one was burned by the British.

"Just think," Eliza said aloud, "everybody is at home now." She frowned. "I wish it could stay this way, with Papa and Richard at home . . . and you!" She flushed, then added, "I even like having Abigail live with us."

"I reckon Richard does too," Jeremiah answered slyly.

Eliza shrugged. "Well, she is the prettiest girl in West Lane School," she said loyally.

"But she can't ride a horse, and she doesn't laugh the way you do, or . . ." Jeremiah faltered, "or think up such grand plans as you, Eliza." Jeremiah was tangled up in his own words, so he stuffed his hands in his pockets and the two continued up the path in silence.

When they arrived at the house Mrs. Bouton had already loaded the table—dried beef, stewed apples, bowls of pickles, chicken and dumplings, potatoes drifting in a sea of fresh butter, rye bread, and milk. Since Father and Richard had come back from the war, breakfast was on the table before the first cock crowed, and the men worked ceaselessly in the fields until the noon meal.

"Richard and I may have to go off again soon," Father had said, so the crops were being planted early.

When everyone had gathered at the table, heads were bowed, and Mr. Bouton began the blessing. Eliza peeked over her folded hands at the little group around the table. Her mother's face, she thought, was serene and beautiful. Abigail's eyes were tightly closed, her cheeks were the color of roses and her dark hair shone as brightly as a blackbird's wings in the sunlight. Luke, pale and thin, looked too old for seventeen. Restlessly, Richard rubbed his clasped fingers across his knuckles. Eliza's eyes rested on Jeremiah's large hands and she thought about his delicate wood carvings and his big boots that continually got into everyone's way under the table. She saw all of these things and said her own silent prayer of thanks.

After the blessing, the hum of conversation, the sound of pewter bowls softly clattering on the tabletop, and the wonderful smells of fresh baked bread, savory chicken, and pungent apples, all came together in a way that made Eliza feel glad to be alive.

Richard was talking about the nest of rabbits he had come upon in the field that morning. "The babies looked so helpless, Papa, I just plowed around the nest," he said.

Mr. Bouton nodded. "I'm the same way. We're too softhearted, Richard. Those babies will grow fat on our young corn."

Eliza was about to ask if there would be peach pie for

desert, but before she could speak the sound of a horse was heard galloping up the road. Mr. Bouton rose from the table and ambled toward the kitchen door. The rest of the family waited silently for the horse and rider to round the house. Visitors at noon were rare, especially now, when all of the men were preoccupied with the war and getting in the spring crops.

Without thinking, Eliza pushed her chair away from the table, but her mother laid a hand on her shoulder. "You must be patient," she said. "We will know who is here in a moment."

Soon they heard the horse trotting back down the lane and Mr. Bouton entered the kitchen carrying a small basket. He was smiling broadly. "It seems," he said, "that a Miss Eliza Bouton received a package at Keeler's Tavern by post today."

Eliza's mouth dropped open. *She* had never been sent a piece of mail!

"The sender of this bundle is so important that Squire Keeler felt compelled to deliver it himself!"

Mr. Bouton lifted Eliza's plate of dumplings from the table with one hand, and with the other he set the basket in front of her. Richard stared. Jeremiah gaped. Abigail's brown eyes opened wide. Eliza gazed at it in wonder.

"You are supposed to open it, child," her father said.

Eliza's fingers trembled as she began to untie the twine that held the basket securely shut. The string dropped down around the basket and she grasped the woven lid on either side and lifted it.

"Ohhhhhh!" Abigail squealed.

"My goodness!" chuckled Mr. Bouton.

The basket was brimming with glistening red silk. Resting on top was a folded sheet of paper, sealed with red

wax. Hastily, Eliza broke the seal and began reading the letter. No one spoke. When she looked up at the faces around the table, tears were shining in her eyes.

"It's from General George Washington!" she quavered.

Richard gulped. "Some on, Sis," he chided, "tell us who it's really from."

"It *is* from General George Washington!" she repeated.

"Well, galloping jackrabbits, Eliza, read the letter out loud!" Jeremiah croaked.

She held the paper between her shaking fingers and squeezed the tears from her eyes so that she could see the writing scrawled across the page.

She read aloud:

April 29, 1777

Dear Miss Eliza Bouton,

Two artfully disguised communications containing information crucial to our war for independence arrived at my headquarters today. Although I am most grateful to all who were involved in their safe delivery, I could not help but think that the young lady who, I am told, carried the messages to Dobbs Ferry would feel somewhat saddened to have lost her red petticoat. So, I am sending you a piece of silk that was given to me by a Frenchman. I hope this crimson material may be fashioned into a new petticoat to replace the one so spiritedly sacrificed by a valiant rebel. And please relay my gratitude to Jeremiah Plunket.

Eliza took a deep breath. "Signed," she said, "General George Washington."

"Well, galloping jackrabbits!" Jeremiah repeated hoarsely.